A PLAGUE OF SPIES

A group of international spies has assembled in the small nation of Alba. Interpol guesses that they aren't there for their holidays — but has no clue as to the real plans being set in motion. Peter Carthage, WAR, Inc.'s slickest agent, is sent to infiltrate and destroy — and ends up captured by an order of most peculiar monks. As Carthage learns the sinister secret of the monastery, he finds himself in the middle of the greatest coup in the history of crime . . .

MICHAEL KURLAND

A PLAGUE
OF SPIES

Complete and Unabridged

LINFORD
Leicester

First published in Great Britain

This Linford Edition
published 2016

A catalogue record for this book is available
from the British Library.

ISBN 978–1–4448–3023–1

Published by
F. A. Thorpe (Publishing)
Anstey, Leicestershire

Set by Words & Graphics Ltd.
Anstey, Leicestershire
Printed and bound in Great Britain by
T. J. International Ltd., Padstow, Cornwall

This book is printed on acid-free paper

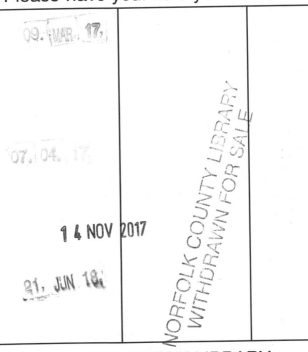

01309 Most probably a spy. He should be
01310 eliminated at the first possible mo
01311 ment, consistent with higher objec
01312 tives. This should be left to Branch
01313 Group A. I scan. I scan. Barb.

1

The black Mercedes sedan made a brief stop before it sped out of Graustark. It then headed south along the Via Claudia, the ancient coastal highway along the Adriatic that, when it leaves the Grand Duchy of Alba and enters Albania, becomes The Glorious Revolutionary Workers' Highway Number One. The car passed under the railroad bridge, rounded the hairpin turn that had become famous to Grand Prix race fans as 'Killer Curve,' and started the climb into the Dinaric Alps. At the speed it was going it would have passed through Alba and reached the Albanian border in twenty-five minutes.

In eighteen minutes, well inside the border, the car left the highway and headed down a steep dirt road toward the shore. It passed the gates of several large, secluded villas, some of which were in existence when Claudius, Emperor and Demigod, spent his summers here to escape the heat and mosquitoes of Imperial Rome.

In a jagged cleft in a mound of bare rock that hung out from the side of the mountain, giving a good view of the road, the watcher sat. A tall, gaunt man with thin blond hair, he was wearing a black leather suit as protection against the daily extremes of weather. He'd been in his perch now for five days.

When the Mercedes turned off the highway, the watcher was interested enough to pick up his binoculars and follow the car. Now, when the car stopped at one particular rusted black gate, the watcher became fascinated. He switched the binoculars for a large spotter's telescope with its tripod jammed into a convenient crack. First he focused on the rear of the car and jotted down the license number in a small, black leather notebook. Then he moved the scope slightly to pick up the car's driver as he got out to use the gate phone.

The driver was of average height, average build, and even — if the statistics are accurate — about average age. He looked to be in his early twenties, and was dressed in a fashion that the watcher put down in his notebook as 'nondescript good.' The watcher, in a neat, square, precise script, wrote down the details he could make out: gray suit — white shirt — black tie — no hat — short hair — black shoes. He snapped a single-lens reflex camera into place over the eyepiece of the scope and focused the ground glass carefully. *Businessman?* he wondered as he waited for the driver to turn around again. *Insurance salesman? Rental agent? Spy? Gangster? Victim?* He shrugged; it was no concern of his. The driver hung up the phone and turned around. The watcher snapped two pictures and then removed the camera and watched as the driver got back into the car. The gate opened and the Mercedes drove through. The gate closed behind the car.

The watcher settled down to wait for the car to come back out. He waited a long time.

*   *   *

Marko drove down the dirt road carefully, examining the gates as he passed them.

When he went by the one with the two stone lions — which, he noticed, both had their noses broken off, giving them a flat-faced look of great dignity — he slowed down. The next gate on the right was the one he was looking for. It was, as had been described to him, built like a portcullis: a stone arch closed by great vertical iron bars. *To protect the castle keep from unwanted visitors*, he decided. *Lucky thing I'm a wanted visitor.* He smiled at a private joke and stopped the car. The house phone was where it was supposed to be, set into a steel panel in the stone. He picked it off the cradle and waited, listening to the distant buzzing through the receiver.

The buzzing stopped. 'Yes?'

'Donald?' Marko asked, as he had been instructed.

'Yes?'

'Mickey sent me.'

There was a pause. 'I'll open the gate,' the voice decided. 'When you drive in, take the road to the left. The right-hand one goes down to the boat dock.'

'Very good,' Marko agreed.

'One never knows,' the voice said obscurely. Marko got back into the car. The rusty iron bars rose slowly out of their slots like a row of jagged teeth, and slammed down behind the car after he drove through.

The road to the left wound around some scrub trees, opened up a beautiful view of the Adriatic, and then ended at the whitewashed expanse of the outer wall of the main house. Marko stopped the car gently and got out by the path that led through a cactus garden to the front door. A short, tubby, bald man waited by the door, his right hand concealed behind him. 'Mickey sent you?' the man asked.

'That's right.' Marko walked up the path, keeping his hands carefully in view. 'He told me to ask you how you liked the butterflies.'

The man laughed, a sound like a band saw cutting across the grain, and brought his hand into view. It held a U.S. Army model .45 caliber automatic, which he stuck between the folds of his stomach and the belt holding up his powder-blue shorts. The paisley sport shirt fell into place to cover it. 'Prettiest butterflies ever,' he said. He stuck out the hand. 'I'm Donald.'

Marko took it stiffly. It was flabby, and the man smelled like a men's locker room. He was not merely bald, but completely shaven, even to the eyebrows. Marko found it faintly repulsive. 'I'm the messenger,' he said, deciding to leave as soon as possible.

'Okay, messenger boy, relax.' Donald laughed again. He could tell that Marko was uncomfortable, but he was amused, not insulted. Most people didn't like him. 'You're a messenger boy, you must have a message. Where's the message?'

Marko took an envelope from the inside pocket of his jacket and handed it to Donald.

'Thanks, boy. You can toddle along now. Or do you want me to sign a receipt?'

'I'm supposed to wait for an answer.'

'That right?' Donald gave him a funny look. 'Okay, come along with me.' He led the way inside the front door, through the inner court, and into a large room off the courtyard.

'Reception room,' Donald said. 'Consider yourself received. I'll have Daisy bring you some tea while you wait.' Marko sat down on a wicker couch, and Donald disappeared through a door, carefully closing the door after him.

* * *

'What is it, John?' Irma Kott asked as her husband entered the kitchen. She wiped her hands on her apron and smiled at him.

'Message from Mickey. It may be what we've been waiting for.'

'That's nice. I'm getting a bit tired of playing the Compleat Hausfrau.'

'Yes,' Kott agreed. 'All this relaxing does get a bit tiring. That reminds me; the messenger is in the living room waiting for an answer. Why don't you bring him some tea?'

'All right. What sort of answer is he waiting for? I thought making up those secret message things took quite some time.'

John Kott shrugged. 'I won't know till I've looked at this one. Remember, when you speak to him — I'm Donald and you're Daisy.'

9

'Daisy,' Irma repeated. 'Silly, but it could be worse.' She started putting tea things on a tray. 'As long as I'm not Brunhilde.'

Kott laughed. 'Give us a kiss, and I'll go see what this thing says.' He embraced her briefly and trotted off down the passage to his office. Once inside, he closed the door behind him, bolted it, and seated himself at a small, secretary-type desk.

The envelope was plain white, legal size, and sealed. On the front the word 'Donald' had been typed. Kott looked it over, carefully checking the gummed flap, which didn't appear to have been tampered with. 'But,' he thought, 'one can never tell.' He slit the envelope open and removed a single sheet of white paper, folded in thirds. This he carefully straightened and laid on the desk. The entire message was neatly typed within the center fold. Thus:

DONALD:
130 13042 13401 8501 115 3528 416
17214 6491 11310 18147 18222 21560
10247 11518 23677 13605 3494 14963

10

98092 5905 11311 10392 10371 0302
21290 5161 39695 23571 17504 11269
18276 18101

Kott turned on a powerful spring-arm
lamp and brought the shielded bulb down
close to the paper. He took a small
magnifying glass on a stand — one of the
sort used by stamp collectors — from a
drawer of the secretary, and positioned
it carefully over the message so that it
focused on the colon after 'Donald.' Then
he bent over and examined the two small
dots. Taking a bottle of colorless fluid
from the drawer, he unstoppered it and
used the glass rod fixed to the stopper to
put one small drop of liquid gently on the
lower dot. For a few seconds nothing happened. Then, as he patiently watched, an
upper layer of the dot came loose and
floated in the drop of liquid.

He carefully unwrapped the tissue
paper from a glass slide and, holding it by
the edges, centered the slide over the dot.
Keeping it perfectly flat, he touched it to
the paper for a second and lifted it. Once
he saw that the dot's upper layer had

deposited itself neatly on the glass, he sighed with satisfaction, turned the slide over, and set it down on the table to dry.

Irma knocked at the door in the one-three-two pattern that she used when she was alone. John stretched and unlocked the door. Irma opened it the least amount that would admit her and slid through. 'What does it say?' she whispered, latching the door behind her.

'I'm about to look,' Kott told her. 'Did you give the messenger boy his tea?'

'Yes.' She smoothed her dress down with her hands. 'He's a nice, clean-cut type.'

The buzz-saw laugh sounded again. 'Executive material,' John agreed, cutting his laugh off as abruptly as he had started it. 'The delivery boy dresses like a vice-president.'

'Don't be unkind. What does the dot say?'

Kott picked up the slide and examined it to make sure it was dry. 'We shall soon see.' From the shelf beside his desk he took a wooden case about two feet long and three inches square. Opening the case, he carefully removed an instrument that looked like a microscope mounted on top of a long tube, and set it upright on the desk by four thin legs that unfolded from the sides of the cylinder. The top of the wooden case held a power cord neatly wound around two pegs. Kott removed this, plugged one end into the tube, and the other into a wall socket. The tube lit up and cast a round blob of light on the table under it.

Kott took the slide and snapped it into place in the microscope stage. The blob of light became fuzzy. He slid a piece of white paper under the tube and focused the light on it. After a moment's fooling with the focusing screw, he brought the image to sharp clarity. It showed a random pattern of short lines and blocks done in stark black.

Irma stared thoughtfully at the image. 'I seem to remember seeing that at the exhibit of modern artists in Graustark three months ago.'

'I remember,' Kott said.

'One could say,' his wife mused, 'that life imitates art. Don't you think?'

Kott snorted. 'One might say that art imitates life, or one might say neither of those asinine things. People have built philosophies on the fact that edelweiss grows only on the top of mountains. Would you pass the decoding glass, please.'

'You have no soul,' Irma declared. 'Where is the what-do-you-call-it?'

'Decoding glass. It's in the top left-hand drawer of the table you're standing next to.'

Irma poked into the indicated drawer and came out with a round leather case like that which is made to hold camera lenses. Kott took it from her, and extracted from it a gadget that looked very much like a camera lens. Opening a slot in the projector tube, he inserted the lens. The jumble of dots and lines on the paper below was immediately changed to a different jumble.

'It doesn't work,' Irma observed.

'I have to align it,' Kott explained.

'How do you align a lens?'

'It's not really a lens,' Kott said, slowly turning the glass in its mount. 'It's a bundle of fiberglass rods that have been arranged to scramble the light going through them.' The pattern on the paper kept changing shape like a monochromatic kaleidoscope as Kott rotated the glass. Suddenly, all at once the dots lined up, and a message appeared. 'There, we're in business.'

Irma bent over to read the message with him. It was short and to the point.

MEETING THURSDAY NEXT. ARRANGEMENTS COMPLETE. BE AT CAFÉ KRANS AT EIGHTEEN HOURS. KILL THE MESSENGER. MICKEY

Kott broke into his laugh again, and the buzz-saw went up and down the scale. Then it turned off. 'So that's why he was to wait for an answer.'

Irma looked distressed. 'He was such a nice boy,' she said.

'You sound like a mother,' Kott said getting up. But he was always a good boy. 'I don't like it either. My mother always wanted me to be a customs agent like my father. Wait here.'

* * *

Marko stood up as the man he knew as Donald came back into the room. 'You took your time,' he observed.

'I did,' Donald agreed. 'I did indeed. But that way I make fewer mistakes.'

'Have you an answer for me to take back?'

'Well,' Donald said, 'I have an answer.'

'What do you mean?'

'I find this annoying and distasteful,' Donald said. 'But I suppose I really shouldn't complain to you.' He pulled a sealed white envelope out of his pocket. 'Here.'

Marko grabbed the envelope and stuffed it into his jacket pocket. 'I'll see that your complaint is passed on.'

'Yes,' Donald said, 'you do that.' He went over to the door and opened it. 'I'll see you out.'

'Thank you,' Marko said stiffly. He left the room and walked slowly through the courtyard. The bald man seemed more solemn than when he had arrived; the furrows in his eyebrowless forehead were more pronounced. Marko found this disconcerting. Fat men shouldn't be serious; it wasn't a good image.

Donald followed him through the courtyard and to the front door. He stood in the doorway while Marko started trudging toward the car.

'Oh, messenger boy!' the bald man called after Marko had taken a few steps.

Marko felt a strong urge to just keep going and not turn around, but he decided he couldn't pretend not to have heard. He turned.

'That's far enough,' the fat man said, tugging the .45 out of his belt.

'What?' Marko saw that the automatic now had a fat tube sticking out from the muzzle. Everything seemed very sharp and clear to him now, and time moved uphill.

That must be a silencer. I always wanted to see one close up, but I guess I never will. He turned on the balls of his feet, and slowly — so slowly — started to run back to the car. *I wonder how they found out,* he thought as his left foot started back to the ground.

A powerful fist struck him on the right side of his back and spun him around. A second fist slammed at his chest under his heart. His hand reached for the spot, and it was wet and sticky. The path touched his head. He had no time to be afraid.

He died.

09964 All Complete. Start motion to form
09965 Branch Group B. Albanian cover
09966 check magnetic drums. I scan. I scan.
09967 Proper stool.

2

It was a cool, bright day, and Peter Carthage felt surprisingly alert and cheerful as he left his Greenwich Village apartment and started the twenty-mile drive to his office in WAR, Inc.'s New Jersey headquarters. It looked, as usual when he left the tunnel and entered Route Twenty, that this was the day that all of northern New Jersey was fleeing north to Manhattan. It also looked, as usual from the size of the traffic jam, that this second Wednesday in September was the day none of them was going to make it.

Peter drove leisurely by the miles of crawling cars and angry drivers until he reached his turnoff. Within five minutes he was driving over the last low hill and in sight of his objective: the parking lot outside WAR, Inc.'s main gate.

The sight this morning that Peter noticed as he started down the hill was different from all other mornings. This morning there were two buses in the parking lot and a mob of America's youth assembled before the gate. The youth came in a variety of sizes, shapes, ages, sexes, dress, and degrees of cleanliness, loudness and intent. They numbered in the whole about fifty. To their side was a smaller mob made up of men of approximately uniform appearance, who seemed to be differentiated only by the presence or absence of varieties of camera equipment around their necks.

Peter parked his car in its slot and got out. 'Aha!' he said softly. 'It is a dissenting time.' He walked over to the gate.

The main crowd, on closer inspection, proved to be made up of teenagers, about two-thirds male and one-third female. Their garb, collectively, was an example of what the well-dressed protester will wear. Sandals were the standard footwear. Above that, the boys wore Levis and a variety of shirts, from khaki to fluorescent. Beards, or attempts at beards, and a summer's worth of uncut hair framed the intent faces. The girls who thought it worthwhile to differentiate themselves from the boys wore miniskirts. The group was sitting on the ground in front of the vehicle entrance to the gate, chanting slogans and waving signs. The chanters seemed to be divided into two major groups, the majority yelling, 'Hell, no — we won't go!' and a loud minority shouting something that sounded like 'More bread, less taxes' — or perhaps it was 'More taxes, less bread,' it was hard to tell. Occasional dissenters were screaming slogans of their own, and a boy near Peter seemed obsessed with a dirty word that he must have recently learned.

The signs were joggling up and down with the rhythm of the chanters like flotsam in a storm. They bore legends like GET OUT OF VIETNAM, MAKE LOVE NOT WAR, DON'T NAPALM CHILDREN, and the boy near Peter carried a neatly printed one that proclaimed THERE'S A WORD FOR IT!

One truck had already been stopped by the human barrier. It was the grocery track, carrying the daily supplies for the lunchroom.

The reporters and photographers were standing in a little cluster waiting for something to happen. The sitters seemed to think that something had already happened, and were content to chant.

'Hi,' Peter greeted the gate guard, who was sitting in his shack having an unconcerned conversation with the driver of the grocery truck. 'What's new?'

The guard waved a hand at the mob. 'Morning, Mister Carthage. Ain't that enough for one day?'

'I suppose,' Peter admitted. 'What are we planning to do about it?'

'Doctor Steadman came out to take a look when the buses arrived, then went back inside without a word. But if I know the Old Man, he'll take care of it without any trouble.'

'I share your faith,' Peter said. 'It'll be interesting to see what he does.' Peter handed the permanent top half of his security badge to the guard, who clipped on the daily-changed bottom half and handed it back. The guard buzzed for the inner gate to open and Peter walked through.

As Peter entered the area, a small panel truck with breakaway sides and the neat legend WEAPONS ANALYSIS AND

RESEARCH, INC. on the side of the door pulled up inside the gate. The driver, Tony Ryan, a plans expert who regularly worked with Peter, waved happily at him. 'Good morning, Peter. I see you're late as usual.'

'I'm nothing if not consistent,' Peter agreed. 'I hope you're not planning to get through that mob out there.'

'Not through them,' Tony said, 'just to them. This truck is our secret weapon.'

'Gosh,' Peter said, 'that must be the death ray with which the evil Doctor Savanna plans to control the world.'

'Right,' Tony agreed. 'Holy moley. Tune in next week for the thrilling conclusion.'

The vehicle gate swung open, and the truck crept slowly forward to meet the sitters. When it had reached the first row, and couldn't advance any further without running over a candidate for the Bearded Lady who sat in the front row of sign-wavers, it stopped. Some of the protesters looked alarmed and started edging in various directions away from the truck.

Tony got out of the driver's seat and went around to the side of the truck. He unlatched one of the sides and rolled it up, revealing a portable snack bar inside. 'Okay kids,' he announced. 'Doctor Steadman, the head of the company, has agreed to speak to you at eleven o'clock. Until then we are to provide you with free coffee and donuts. Enjoy yourselves.'

The protesters looked as if someone had just pulled a very dirty trick on them. It had never occurred to them that the head of WAR, Inc. might be willing to talk to them, and the free food and drink seemed like an additional insult. They weren't being taken seriously. Most of them just sat and sulked and muttered warnings to the few that stood up to take advantage of the offer.

Peter smiled and walked away. He decided to be on hand when Doctor Steadman came out to speak — it should be worth watching.

Peter found a note waiting for him that said that Doctor Steadman wanted to see him as soon as he came in. He straightened his tie and went to the Old Man's office.

Miss Cow, Doctor Steadman's private

secretary, looked up sadly when Peter walked in. 'You're late as usual,' she said. 'Hand in your secret decoder ring; you're through.'

'No,' Peter said in mock alarm, 'not the secret decoder ring. Anything but that.'

'If I thought you meant that . . . ' Miss Cow sighed. 'Go on inside, he's waiting for you.'

Doctor Thomas Steadman, Founder and President of WAR, Inc., was seated behind his massive oak desk. In the red leather chair to the right of the desk sat a man who was engaged in heavy conversation with Doctor Steadman.

'Ah, Peter,' Steadman said, looking up as Peter walked in. 'Good afternoon.'

Peter sighed. 'A man comes in five minutes late because he can't get through the unbridled crowds outside the gates, and all he meets is sarcasm. Good afternoon to you, sir.'

'I'd like you to meet this gentleman,' Doctor Steadman said. 'He's joining our organization. Peter Carthage, Theodore Ursa.'

'Glad to have you with us,' Peter said,

walking forward and extending his hand.

Ursa stood up, uncoiling from the chair and towering over Peter's six-foot frame. 'My pleasure.' He grasped Peter's hand firmly. A tall, solid, black man with a handsomely chiseled face, he gave an impression of controlled power.

Doctor Steadman also stood up. 'I had planned to talk to both of you, since you're going to be working together almost immediately, but it seems I have to prepare to meet our young guests. Go away somewhere and get to know each other, and I'll talk to you later. Here — ' He slid a file folder with URSA, THEODORE typed across the corner over to Peter. ' — basic information.'

Peter picked up the folder. 'Let's go over to the lunchroom and talk over coffee,' he suggested.

And so they did. Theodore, after insisting that he be called Ted, stared politely into his coffee while Peter read the personnel folder. It was quite impressive in a starkly factual way. Theodore Ursa grew up in Georgia, graduated from Harvard University, went into the Army as a second lieutenant in the Civil Affairs Department, served four years, and then was discharged for medical reasons with the rank of captain.

'Captain in four years,' Peter said. 'You must have friends in high places.'

Ted shrugged. 'I think it's more due to the high accident rate.'

'Were you in combat?'

'That's a matter of definition, I suppose. I was in Vietnam. They didn't call it combat, but a lot of us were getting killed pretty regular. I was an adviser to the Civil Police Force, and Victor Charlie thought he could do without me.'

'I believe it,' Peter said. 'Discharge for medical reasons. Were you wounded?'

'Lost a leg,' Ted said, slapping somewhere below his right knee. 'This one's aluminum.'

'Really?' Peter asked in surprise. 'You handle it beautifully; I never would have noticed.'

'Oh, it serves all right for most things. I walk fine, dance pretty good. It's not too handy for all-out running, but I gave up the high hurdles after college.'

'How'd it happen?' Peter asked. 'That is, if you don't mind talking about it. Just my morbid curiosity.'

Ted sipped his coffee. 'Stupidity,' he said. 'Sheer stupidity. And not even my own stupidity — which, God knows, there's enough of — but someone else's. We were walking down this road on early morning patrol when this guy next to me sees a wooden box sitting on the side of the road. 'Hey, look,' he calls, 'someone's dug up a 'Cong landmine.' Next thing I know, he kicks it. Blam. I wake up the next day in a field hospital minus one leg. Only I hadn't gone to sleep quite that fast; it took half an hour for a medic to get there and give me a shot of morphine. I understand I was screaming most of that time, but I don't remember. I don't particularly want to.'

'You mean this soldier knew it was a landmine before he kicked it?'

'He did. He didn't know anything at all after.'

Peter shook his head. 'What the hell would possess anyone to do a thing like that?'

29

'We'll never know,' Ted said. 'But I must admit, I've wondered from time to time.'

'You'd better keep your aluminum leg out of the Old Man's clutches,' Peter said. 'He's a gadgeteer, and he'd probably love to rig up an artificial limb with all sorts of contraptions and compartments.'

Ted laughed. 'Thanks for the warning. I keep a pint flask of bourbon down there, and that's all I want.' He took a big bite into what the waitress had warned them was yesterday's donut, the fresh supply being held up at the gate, and washed it down with coffee. 'Any other words of advice for the new employee? I do so want to make good my first day on the job.'

'What the firm's interested in is brains,' Peter said. 'And I think you'll do fine.'

'Why, thank you,' Ted said. 'That's very kind. Any idea what this job we're going to be working together on is all about?'

'I was going to ask you the same thing. I guess we'll have to wait until this afternoon. In the meantime, I'm going to go watch Herr Doktor Professor Steadman attempt to communicate with our younger generation. If you have nothing better to do . . . '

Ted stood up. 'My pleasure.'

★　★　★

The lecture hall was already full of protesters when Peter and Ted took their place in the back of the room. The assembled youths were busy scratching, squirming, and chanting. This time, there seemed to be a general agreement as to what to yell. *No more war!* was being loudly beat out to the timing of stamping feet. *No more war, no more war,* like an arena of witch doctors gathered to stamp the devils out of a particularly reticent case of malaria.

Doctor Steadman climbed up on the stand in front of the hall, and stood behind the lectern facing his audience. Instead of dying down, the chanting increased in intensity. Doctor Steadman attempted to say something into the microphone, but even the loudspeakers couldn't raise his voice over the yelling. He smiled and, calmly sitting down behind the lectern, started to slowly and methodically fill his pipe and light it. The yelling went on for some time, but when it became evident that no one else was going to get up and attempt to speak while the noise continued, it gradually died down. When only six or seven people were left to chant, it abruptly stopped, as though none of the protesters wanted to take the chance of being left to chant alone.

Doctor Steadman stood up. The chanting started again, but ceased when he looked like he was going to sit down again. When the noise had stopped, Doctor Steadman looked over his audience.

'Good morning,' he said over the microphone. A few of the youths, probably from college habit, returned the greeting. They were glared at by their fellows. The members of the press, gathered to the right of the hall, started writing. 'My name is Thomas Steadman. I'm the president of Weapons Analysis and Research, Incorporated.' He paused and looked around at the assemblage. 'Did you want to speak with me?'

There was an uncomfortable silence.

'Have you a spokesman?'

One of the crowd, who seemed a little older than most, stood up and glared at Doctor Steadman. 'We're against war,' he stated.

Doctor Steadman regarded the bearded youth. 'Very succinct,' he said. 'May I ask your name?'

'Lester Borely.'

'Thank you, Mister Borely. Would you like to continue?'

Lester looked around him for support, and then squared off at the platform. 'The war in Vietnam is evil,' he announced, 'and the draft is a crime.'

Steadman leaned over the rostrum. 'I tend to agree with you.'

Lester looked shocked. Another youth jumped up and pointed a finger at the stand. 'You call yourselves War, Incorporated!' he yelled.

'That's true, son,' Doctor Steadman agreed. 'Therefore, you assume we must be in favor of war?'

'Aren't you?' the youth demanded.

'Do you think the American Cancer

Society is in favor of cancer?' Steadman asked. 'Would you assume that the League for Crippled Children goes around crippling children?'

There was a mutter in the audience as the protesters tried to decide what to make of this.

'I believe war is the greatest evil possible in today's world,' Doctor Steadman told his audience. 'I find myself in disagreement with the conduct of the fighting in Vietnam, although I'm sure my views are not yours. I also think the draft should be abolished. We do, of course, need an army, but I'm in favor of a professional army, not a force made up of draftees.'

'Why do we need an army?' the youth asked.

'Some people have a habit of taking what doesn't belong to them; that's why we need a police force. Some countries have the same habit.'

'Why do you call yourselves War, Incorporated?' Lester asked.

'We concern ourselves with the theory and practice of war,' Doctor Steadman said, 'just as a police force must concern itself with the theory and practice of crime. This doesn't mean we're in favor of war. On the contrary, we will do anything in our power to prevent war.

'Now we come to the interesting question: What will prevent war?' Doctor Steadman looked intently at his audience. 'I'm sure you all have theories about that.' Another murmur made its round. This one seemed appreciative. 'Let me tell you what we believe, and what we're doing about it.

'First we must consider what causes war. The best way to do this is to look into history and see what has caused wars in the past. Any ideas?'

A few hands went up. Peter leaned over to Ted and whispered, 'He's turning a hostile audience into a lecture course. Got to give the Old Man credit.'

Doctor Steadman pointed to one of the raised hands and its owner stood up. 'Economic imbalance,' he said.

'You mean, somebody has something and somebody else wants it?' Doctor Steadman asked.

The boy nodded.

'That's good, and you're right; that's the basic cause of war. But the want doesn't have to be economic. The holy crusades are an example of somebody wanting a bit of land, not for its economic, but its symbolic, value. Then there are ideological wars. The American Civil War was fought over the two ideas of states' rights and slavery. This is still an example of somebody wanting something. It's like two men fighting over a belief. The statement would be something like, 'I'm going to keep beating on him till he admits I'm right.' Ideological wars usually look silly to observers several hundred years after the event, when the point of dispute has long been settled and forgotten. The religious wars in Europe in the Middle Ages look like examples of mass insanity in today's world of religious toleration. But the issues were important and valid to the people who fought and died for them.

'Then there are wars that are both economic and ideological. World War II is a good example of this. Hitler wanted to take over the western world. The Japanese military clique, with their 'Far Eastern Greater Co-Prosperity Sphere,' wanted the other half. Hitler also wanted to establish a Fascist dictatorship and to eliminate certain 'racially undesirable' people, such as the Jews, the Gypsies, the Poles, the Czechs, the Russians, and everyone else who wasn't what he called 'Aryan.' The rest of the world didn't want to be either taken over or eliminated, so we had a war.

'Today — ' Doctor Steadman looked around him. ' — you see, I do eventually come to the point — today the world is faced with a series of problems, both economic and ideological, of a type that have always in the past led to war. But today, for the first time in history, a war of direct confrontation between the two principals in the ideological-economic conflict is unthinkable. Both sides possess the ability to destroy the other even after they themselves have been attacked and, for all practical purposes, destroyed. The leaders on both sides of this divided world realize this; and, being intelligent, moral men, will do everything in their power to see that this doesn't happen.

'But the confrontation continues. And, on a lesser level, occasionally becomes a military problem. You all know the examples of this: Greece, Malaya, Korea, and Vietnam are probably the best-known. Whatever you think of Vietnam, you must recognize it for what it is, an indirect military confrontation of today's two great powers.

'Now, to what we do here. Despite the polarization of the world into two great power areas, there still many small countries in the world. As a matter of fact, there are more today than there have ever been. These people have their own problems. Problems which, unfortunately, the two great powers are only too willing to try to resolve. If one of these powers — say, the Soviet Union, or Communist China — sticks its nose in, then the other side — perhaps the United States or Great Britain — soon finds itself involved up to the elbows.

'The thing that tends to be overlooked in today's two-power world is that acts of political, ideological, or economic aggrandizement are just as possible on a small scale as on a large. Small countries need to be able to protect themselves from their small neighbors. The tendency, quite logically, is for the small country to ask one of the superpowers for this protection. The trouble with this, as will be immediately obvious to you, is twofold. First of all: the great power quite logically wants something in return for its assistance. This could be either bases or political alignment. Second: it's a safe bet that as soon as one of the great powers lines up on one side of such a conflict, the other power will feel compelled to come in on the other side. This is the polarization process. The great danger of such a process is that if it ever gets out of control, the two great powers will find themselves in a direct confrontation. Then we find ourselves thinking about the unthinkable, as such a confrontation could lead to World War III.

'What this small country usually needs, to discourage outside aggression or internal subversion, is advice and training for its armed forces. When a country is able to take care of itself, it usually discourages neighbors from trying to take care of it in their own way.

'I don't mean to claim that all our jobs are as important as this. We handle training of paramilitary forces down to the level of local police. But I do claim that we have a highly developed sense of morality as far as the jobs we will take. If a government wants you to train and equip their army, it's fairly easy to tell what they have in mind. For example: if they're very interested in having units trained for river crossing, and there are no rivers in the country, they're thinking of more than home defense.'

A girl stood up in the audience. 'What you're saying,' she said, 'is that you end war by training people to fight and kill. That doesn't sound logical to me.'

'You put it strongly, young lady, but that is just about what I'm saying. You can't end war by ignoring it and hoping it will go away, any more than you can end disease by pretending that there's no such thing as smallpox. You must be on the lookout for it and be ready to stamp it out and prevent it from spreading.'

A few, though by no means all, of the listeners were unconsciously nodding in agreement with what Doctor Steadman was saying. Peter turned to Ted. 'It looks like the Old Man might make a few converts.'

'They seem to be impressed with his sincerity,' Ted commented.

'Oh, he believes what he's saying, all right. I've heard variants of this speech too often before to doubt that. Let's go have lunch.'

'I wonder what he's got in mind for us?' Ted said as they stood up to leave.

'We won't be wondering much longer,' Peter said. 'But one thing I know; big or small, it'll be interesting.'

3

The French police received word that Benjy the Mug was in France almost as soon as he arrived. The only problem was that they couldn't seem to find him. Interpol sent the file on Benjamin Drommer on from Turkey, where he had last been seen, along with word that he was headed for Paris. Various police informants in the Paris area reported that his name was being mentioned by those people who have reason to know about such things. The informants, unfortunately, couldn't supply anything about his appearance, whereabouts, or intentions.

The Interpol file was very little help. It contained only a ten-year-old description, some badly-taken fingerprints, and a list of bank robberies, jewel heists, and armored car stickups that Benjy was known or believed to have masterminded.

The initial reaction of the French police was disbelief at the size of the list.

They called Istanbul for further information.

'Nothing further is definitely known,' the Turkish authorities replied. 'However, it is believed . . . ' And a longer list of improbably audacious crimes was appended. Queries to the British, Italian, American, and Japanese authorities merely extended the list. No one had a recent picture of him. No one could supply information on modus operandi or probable habits. No one wanted him back if he could be caught.

'Put a double guard around whatever he's after,' the Italians suggested.

'Have no idea what he's after,' the French answered.

'Guard everything!' the Italians insisted.

This was too much. The French replied, with lofty Gallic assurance, that they could handle Benjy the Mug. They subtly stepped up their efforts to find him.

Three weeks after his reported arrival, an armored car going from Marseilles to Paris failed to arrive. It was found the next day on the side of the road: blown up, opened, and empty. The police put their experts to work on it. It was determined that the car had been stopped by a bazooka shell. A scientific examination of the car revealed nothing further.

Two weeks later, an armored car returning to Paris from a branch bank in Dijon failed to arrive. It was never found.

Four weeks after this, six men held up a diamond cooperative in Paris, keeping nine diamond merchants and fourteen customers prisoners for forty minutes while an impregnable safe was opened and emptied.

'Aha!' the French police said. 'He has a gang.'

A month went by with nothing happening. The police collated their information and discovered that no matter how many times you add zeros, you still come up with zero. Then they got a hint. An informant whispered that he had heard from a friend that another friend had a cousin who knew a man who might be able to tell the name of one of the men who had gathered in the diamonds with Benjy the Mug.

Two more weeks passed while they followed this lead. Then came the unkindest cut of all. Benjy, with his gang increased to twelve, walked into the main branch of the *Credit Allemagne*, one of France's oldest international banks, at one in the afternoon, and removed from it four million francs' worth of gold bullion that had been received in a secret shipment that morning.

Two days later, the police managed to apprehend the man who had been named by the person who knew the man with the cousin with the friend who had first been mentioned by their informant. After several hours in a back room of the police station, they had succeeded in extracting an address from him.

Within an hour, a small house in a quiet suburb of Paris was surrounded by police. After some pounding on the door, the inspector in charge discovered that it was unlocked. Within a few minutes, he had further established that the house was empty. The police set about searching the house. In an upstairs closet, they found a war-surplus bazooka. In another location, due to the efficiency of French police and the inefficiency of French plumbing, they found three water-soaked fragments of paper.

The police laboratory went to work on the fragments. One of them proved to say '*ting job. I thi*'. Another stated '*ll be worth at le*'. The third said '*eet in Graustark on Thu*'.

The French police sat back, relaxed, sighed, and washed their hands. They sent a Letter of Information through Interpol to the Minister of Police, Grand Duchy of Alba. It contained a file that was notable only for the paucity of information it held.

11616 Against Alba should proceed as soon
11617 as

4

Peter Carthage sprawled comfortably out on a canvas beach chair, with his legs dangling over the edge, and dug his toes into the warm sand. 'Behold the beautiful Adriatic,' he said, gesturing toward the deep blue water in front of him, 'playground of royalty.'

Ted Ursa, draped over an identical chair to Peter's left, just grunted without opening his eyes. But Professor Perlemutter, third member of the WAR, Inc. crew in the Grand Duchy of Alba, rolled over and sat up. The yard and a half of bright yellow bathing suit that covered his corpulent middle glittered brightly as he moved. 'I might retire and spend my old age here,' he commented. 'My 'Golden Years,' as the advertising euphemists so cleverly put it.'

'If you keep that bathing suit, you could rent yourself out as a heliograph,' Peter told him. 'Signal ships at sea for a distance of up to five miles. What's that thing made of, metal fiber?'

'I believe this costume is fiberglass,' the Professor said. 'It was designed to reflect light, and thus stay cool. I find it quite comfortable.'

Ursa opened one eye and glanced over. 'Ow!' he said. 'The glare hurts. Professor, can't you turn that damn thing off?'

'I am not used,' Perlemutter informed them, 'to being ridiculed about my appearance.' He settled back down into the canvas, which bulged under his weight.

'No comment,' Peter said. He rolled over to make sure he was getting evenly done, while wondering about the philosophic difference between himself on the beach and a roast in the broiler. It was a matter of intent, he decided.

'I think we had better gather our rosebuds while we may,' Professor Perlemutter said from the midst of his chair. 'We're not supposed to be here on a vacation, you know. I imagine they'll want us to start earning our money sometime soon.'

'I think it's a mark of highest consideration and regard for our professional ability. We arrive here on a Thursday, get immediately taken to one of the best hotels in Alba, and are told that the Minister of Police will see us on Monday. Obviously they wanted us to have a little vacation before we started our examination of the police force, to get us in a better mood. I think it would be ungrateful of us not to take the fullest advantage of it.'

'Speaking of rosebuds . . . ' Ted said, staring straight ahead. Peter turned to look. There, on a line that passed fifteen feet in front of them, angling toward the water, ran a girl. Wearing the briefest of bathing scraps, head held tall, feet high-stepping in a rhythmic motion, blonde hair waving in time with her feet, she proudly jogged past them. About ten feet behind her jogged another girl. Behind the second, there was a third. Behind the third, a fourth. Peter stopped counting after twenty-seven, and just enjoyed watching the undulating line passing in front of him. The girls jogged on to a spot further down the beach, where they formed up into rows. A woman, somewhat older and more managerial-looking than the rest, strode out to the bikini-filled square with a small case in her hands. 'All right, girls,' she said, putting the case down on the sand. Rhythmic music emanated from the case, and the woman clapped her hands in time with the sound.

'A portable radio,' Ted commented, watching the display of young woman-hood with interest.

'Certainly a tape recorder,' Peter judged, gazing in the same direction.

'One, two, three, four,' the woman called above her clapping. The girls went into an intricate series of calisthenic maneuvers involving hips, legs, trunk, head, and arms, each part being considered and exercised separately.

'Excuse me,' a low, throaty voice said. Peter turned. A woman was sitting on the lounge chair in the cabana next to theirs. She must have arrived while the attention of the men was focused on the display of girlish charms down the beach. She was herself, Peter saw, fully worthy of receiving all the attention a man might care to focus on her. With soft brown hair tied behind her, and a subdued bathing suit that promised rather than revealed, her firm, well-kept body was that of the sort of beautiful woman the girls down the beach might turn into in five or ten years if they were lucky.

'Yes?' Peter asked, trying not to stare.

'Purely in the interest of furthering your dispassionate quest for knowledge,' she said with the hint of a chuckle in her voice, 'the machine is a record player.'

Professor Perlemutter stirred. 'Ah, thank you, madam,' he said. 'That hadn't occurred to me, as I didn't see anyone open the contraption to put a record in.'

'It's a new sort of machine,' the woman explained. 'You don't have to open it. You just slide the record into a slot in the side. It's very convenient as long as you keep it sand-free. Sand seems to gum up the works.'

'I see,' Perlemutter said. 'One more question, if you don't mind, madam. Do you know the, eh, function of this musical exercising? What is it, some sort of rhythmic karate?'

The woman laughed. 'It's far more strenuous than karate. It's dance. The girls are members of a dance troupe. They go through two hours of exercise every morning before they start rehearsing. Then they spend the rest of the day practicing routines. That is, unless there's a show. Then they only practice half the day.'

'It sounds very arduous,' Peter said.

'It is, it is. They don't get paid half enough, just ask any of them.'

Peter looked back over to where the girls were bouncing to music. 'What troupe is it?'

'The Maggi Blaire dancers.'

'Oh, yes; I've seen them. They're very good.'

'Why, thank you,' the woman said.

Ted asked, 'Are you part of the troupe?'

'Sort of. I'm Maggi Blaire.'

'Ah!' the Professor said. 'You're the one who overworks and underpays these girls, and then takes all the credit for their dancing.'

'That's right.' Maggi laughed. 'And we nurse and chaperone them. Keep them out of trouble and teach them to dance. I also pick their clothing for them, show them how to use makeup, and write letters home to their parents assuring them that the little darlings are all right. It manages to keep me busy.'

'Welcome,' Peter said. 'It's a pleasure to share a beach with you. Are you going to be here long?'

'About two weeks. There are two Wednesday-night galas coming up. The social events of the season. They're for charity, of course. We're one of the feature acts.'

'Wonderful,' Ted said, looking at the girls. 'I hope we're able to see the show.'

'Are you here on business?' Maggi asked.

'That's right,' Peter said. 'We're supposed to be making a study of the Alba police force; recommending improvements and the like.'

'Oh, you're policemen.'

'Not exactly,' Peter said. 'But close enough.'

'Well. It's a pleasure to meet you. That

54

is, it would be if you'd tell me your names.'

Professor Perlemutter attempted to bow from a sitting position and almost upset his chair. 'Allow me to introduce us,' he said, righting the chair and himself. 'The gentleman closest to you is Peter Carthage. Next in the row is Theodore Ursa. And I am Professor Perlemutter. Your servants, madam.'

'Well,' Maggi said. She stood up and went into a deep curtsey. 'Your slave, good sirs. I can do no less.'

'A woman who understands the graces,' Professor Perlemutter said. 'A very rare thing to find these days. Girls these days smoke, and drink, and go around unchaperoned wearing short skirts, and all sorts of things.'

Peter nodded his head in joking agreement. 'Disgraceful, I calls it.'

'You shock me, sirs,' Maggi said. 'Why, how can such things happen in this enlightened age? Why, this is the twentieth century!'

'Shocking,' Ted agreed. 'I shall write a letter to the *Times* about it.'

'My astrology chart told me I was

going to meet some interesting people today,' Maggi said. 'I'm glad it's come through for a change.'

'You, ah, follow astrology?' Professor Perlemutter asked.

'Certainly. It could surprise you. What sign are you?'

'Gemini,' the Professor said.

'Pisces,' Peter volunteered.

Ted sighed. 'I never had a sign. We were too poor.'

One of the liveried minions of the Hotel Caligula trotted down the beach toward them and stopped in front of the cabana. 'Mister Carthage?'

'Yes,' Peter admitted.

'The Prefect of Police called. He wonders if you and your friends could meet with him this afternoon in his office.' He announced it with the condescending air of one who considers the police far down on the social ladder. He could have been informing them that someone wanted to see them about their garbage.

'Thank you,' Peter said. The minion sniffed and trotted away.

'It's only Sunday. I wonder what he

wants us for?' Professor Perlemutter asked.

'It must be an unsolved murder,' Maggi said. 'How exciting. You must come back and tell me all about it. After you've tracked the criminal to his lair, of course.'

'Of course,' Peter agreed. 'If you'll excuse us, we must go and get our tape measures and magnifying-glasses.'

'Splendid,' Maggi said. 'I do hope the butler didn't do it.'

★   ★   ★

The Prefecture of Police was the largest building in Graustark, and quite the largest in the whole Duchy of Alba. It was brownstone, seven stories high, and built around the turn of the century. The circular elevator that rose up the middle of the stairwell, although ancient and creaky, was obviously an afterthought. The Prefect's office on the top floor was mellowed oak, with the deep glass of many polishings. Its hardwood floor was worn by the feet of many past prefects. The gentleman who now held that office paced in the grooves cut by his predecessors.

'I apologize for interrupting your Sunday,' he said. 'But a matter of the utmost concern has come up, and I feel that we can use your services.'

'Of course, Prefect Damarat,' Professor Perlemutter rumbled from the depths of the armchair he had settled himself in. 'We are at your disposal to help in any way feasible.'

'Yes, and I thank you,' the Prefect said. 'We have a quite adequate police force here for the type of thing we are called upon to handle. British and French experts set up the system we follow in nineteen hundred and one; and at that time, it was the most modern on the continent. We were the second police force in Europe to use finger-prints for identification. But now . . . ' Damarat shrugged, his arms wide. ' . . . it's beyond me. It seems that even the function of our department is changing. Or, perhaps, just broadening. It is now necessary to be aware of factors that we could once ignore.' Damarat paused and looked around to see if his audience was following him.

'If you don't mind my asking, sir, what

sort of factors do you mean?' Peter asked.

'Aha!' Damarat settled behind his desk and pushed his wire-rim glasses more firmly up on the bridge of his nose. 'That's what I mean. That's exactly what I mean.' He took a notebook out of his desk. 'The regular police concerns that I'm sure you're familiar with: murder, robbery, burglary, arson, extortion, and the like; these we can take care of quite adequately. We've had plenty of experience. At least once a year, an attempt is made to hold up or burglarize the Casino d'Alba. Never has such an attempt succeeded. At the job of being policemen, we are quite proficient.

'But now it is not enough to be policemen. We are also Alba's army, navy, and border guards. At that, we have not so much experience. Also, despite the fact that the Grand Duchy of Alba is a country without a foreign policy and quite without secrets, we are infested with spies. The police department is going to have to set up a counterespionage department.' Damarat pushed at his glasses again. 'Isn't that the silliest thing you ever heard? Alba with a counterspy department.'

Professor Perlemutter rubbed his hands together and stared musingly at the ceiling. 'It isn't altogether without precedent,' he said. 'The German Federal Police have their Section K; Scotland Yard has the Special Branch; the FBI has a counterintelligence branch; the *Sûreté* has the *Deuxième Bureau*. Most countries leave their internal security in the hands of the police.'

'Yes, yes. Of course. I know that. But most countries are big enough and important enough to have secrets.' Damara riffled through his notebook. 'The question is not whether such a department should be attached to the police, but why Alba should need it at all.'

'Fair enough,' Peter said. 'Why do you think Alba needs a counterintelligence department?'

'Strange things are happening in Alba, Mister Carthage. Strange things. You know, of course, that Graustark has for many years been the meeting place of half the spies in Europe?'

'I've heard stories,' Peter said.

Ted Ursa leaned forward in his chair.

'But I understood that the main reason they came here was that it was a sort of neutral ground.'

'That's true,' Damarat said. 'Or, that has been true for years. They came to Alba because it was a place they could spend their money without accounting, and without worrying that some competitor might think they were after something of value in the way of information. In Alba, of course, there would be no information of value unless they brought it in themselves. It is true that Graustark became a sort of information trading center, but that was nothing to concern us. The most casual police surveillance was enough to keep these people in line. The thing they didn't want was to draw attention to themselves. These are, you understand, mostly what are called low-level agents: the amateurs and freelance specialists who sell what they have to the highest bidder. No, they caused us no trouble.'

Professor Perlemutter nodded. 'I see. That's how it was then. I take it that it isn't that way any more.'

'The situation has changed,' Damarat

agreed. 'The trouble is, we're not sure of exactly how it has changed.' He waved the notebook in the air. 'This contains the reports collected over the past few months on the known espionage agents in Alba. Up until two months ago, it reads normally. Then it starts getting strange.'

Ted Ursa stirred and looked interested. 'Strange? That's fascinating. How so, strange?'

'Well,' Damarat said, looking faintly embarrassed, 'if it was anything definite, I wouldn't have to call it strange, would I? These people are behaving differently, and I have no idea why. They're starting to act in a manner I can only describe as sneaky. They're going to secret meetings, passing secret messages, using passwords, and in general behaving like spies. It's making us very nervous. I know how silly that sounds — our spies are behaving like spies — but, as of this morning, it isn't funny anymore.'

Professor Perlemutter shifted in his chair. 'How's that, sir?' he asked.

Damarat pushed a button on his desk and leaned back in his chair. He surveyed the three faces in front of him. 'We made one attempt at counterespionage. It was ill-advised. A young man, a native Alban who had been away to college in France, came home to Graustark and joined the police force. Since he'd been away for five years and wasn't known here, we put him on special assignment. He managed to become a courier in the spy organization — that is, if it is an organization; we're not even sure of that. We made arrangements to get copies of every message he carried. They were all in code, and we haven't been able to read any of them yet, although we're still trying.' Damarat gripped the edge of his desk. His knuckles showed white under the strain. 'This morning, the boy's body washed ashore on a rocky section of the coast. It was found by a family of Italian tourists who were going out for an early morning swim. There were two bullet holes in it.'

Damarat's secretary, a thin, large-headed man with a bristle mustache and a military bearing, entered in response to his boss's ring.

'Yes, sir,' he said, standing stiffly at attention.

'Has Mister Smith arrived?'

'Yes, sir. He's waiting downstairs. He doesn't seem to like waiting.'

'Fetch him up here,' Damarat instructed.

'Yes, sir.' The secretary did a precise about-face and marched out the door.

'You run your police in a very military manner,' Peter observed.

'My secretary runs himself in a military manner; it's not of my doing.'

'That's a shame about that boy,' Ted said. 'Have you any idea who did it?'

'We know who he was going to see last time he reported in. He had a message to deliver, and we copied it as usual. But we don't even know for sure that he ever delivered it.'

'It does sound as if you have a problem,' Professor Perlemutter said. 'When someone resorts to murder to conceal his actions, it is safe to assume that his actions are reprehensible.'

'The murder — or, rather, the discovery of the body — is what seemed urgent enough to call you on Sunday. But that's just the first problem. There are a few other things I'm worried about that I'd like to talk over with you, but they'll keep.'

There was a knock on the door, and the secretary stepped inside. 'Mister Smith to see you, sir.'

'Show him in,' Damarat directed.

'Yes, sir.' The secretary managed to refrain from saluting.

Mister Smith was tall and bony. His age was indeterminate, somewhere between forty and seventy. His close-cropped hair showed strong traces of the original blond through the gray. He possessed a strong reservoir of nervous energy and an intense, dominating manner. Unconsciously accenting the secretary's manner, he marched into the room and stopped precisely three paces before the desk.

'Prefect Damarat,' he snapped. 'Good of you to see me.'

'It's an honor to meet you,' Damarat said, standing and extending his hand. 'Your reputation precedes you.'

Smith took the hand and gave it a short up-and-down motion. 'You expected me?'

'The British Consul said you might be dropping in,' Damarat explained.

'Yes, of course.'

'Please sit down,' Damarat said, waving to a chair.

'I'd prefer to stand, thank you.'

'As you wish. Gentlemen, let me present to you Mister, er, Smith, of British Intelligence. These are Messieurs Perlemutter, Carthage, and Ursa of War, Incorporated. They're here to aid me in a little problem we have.'

Smith examined them, setting each face firmly in his memory as he looked at it. 'A pleasure. I've heard of your organization, of course.'

'Mister Smith,' Peter said, extending his hand and receiving the perfunctory shake. 'I've heard a bit about your organization, too.'

'Yes,' Smith said. 'Amazing the way intelligence groups are turning into publicity organizations, isn't it? It doesn't seem to matter what you do anymore; it's what the people at home think you've done that's important.'

'What can we here in Alba do for you, Mister Smith?' Damarat asked.

Smith gave a very tight-lipped smile. 'I

may surprise you. I think, actually, that I can help you. Perhaps I should say that we may be able to help each other.'

'How is that, sir?' Professor Perlemutter asked.

'Unless I am mistaken,' Smith said with the air of a man who is seldom mistaken, 'you have a problem here in Alba. As a matter of fact, you are fast developing two apparently separate problems. Is that right?'

'Well . . .'

'The first problem could be described as a plague of spies. Something which I'm sure is quite new to Alba.'

Damarat leaned back with his fingers laced together and stared at his visitor. 'It's something quite new to Alba.'

'Well, when you play host to a dangerous animal as long as you have been, you shouldn't be surprised when you finally get bitten.'

'That's unfair!' Damarat protested.

'Is it? Perhaps. The second problem involves an influx of criminals, types quite distinct from the low-level agents: bank robbers, heist men, the sort of men who aren't afraid to use any available weapon to commit any possible crime.'

'You seem to know quite a bit about our affairs, Mister Smith.'

Smith looked annoyed.

'Not at all. As it happens, I know a lot about the affairs of the men in question. You've been considering these as two problems, but I'm here to tell you that the two things are related.'

Damarat nodded. 'I see. I've just been telling my colleagues here about the first problem you mentioned, because it seemed more immediate at the moment. The influx of heavy-type criminals is something that we've become aware of, but can't do anything about. These men haven't broken any laws that we know of. No country has asked us to extradite them. We just keep receiving dossiers from Interpol saying that so-and-so, who has just entered Alba, has a suspect record of doing everything from stealing the Eiffel Tower to plugging all the toilets in the Hotel Metropole. But a suspect record isn't proof. We can just let them stay and spend money, and try to keep a close watch on them while they're here.

Word must be going around in criminal circles that Alba is a good place to get away from it all.'

'You think that's all they're here for — rest and relaxation?' Damarat shrugged.

'What else? What have we got to interest them? The casino? If they think they can figure out a successful way to rob it, they're welcome to try. It's tempted a lot of people before in the past eighty years, and none of them has gotten away with a centime.'

'The, ah, casino is the only thing worth robbing in Alba?' Professor Perlemutter asked, leaning forward.

'It's the most tempting prize. There are at all times over five million American dollars' worth of assorted currencies on hand at the casino. There are also a few other things that might tempt a crook, the sort of things that are found around any large gambling establishment. First, naturally, the hotel rooms of the people who come to the casino. There's a fortune in jewels visible in the dining room of either of the main hotels every night during the season.

'Then there are the jewelers. Many of the important jewelry stores of New York, Paris, and London maintain branches here.'

'People come here to buy jewelry?' Peter asked.

'Not exactly,' Ted answered for Damarat. 'Although sometimes a big winner may wish to reward his wife — or whatever woman was standing by while he played — by buying her a little diamond trinket. The point is that sometimes a player might be put in a position where he desires to sell some jewelry — and quickly.'

'That makes sense,' Peter acknowledged.

'That's it exactly,' said Damarat. 'The interesting thing is to watch someone who has paid thirty thousand dollars for a bracelet arguing with the jeweler's representative for only offering him ten to buy it back. People never seem to realize that there's as big a markup on gems as there is on anything else that is bought wholesale and sold retail.'

'What's even more interesting,' said Ted, who seemed to have had some experience along this line, 'is to watch the face of a man who paid forty thousand dollars for a diamond being told that it's a doublet, and only worth a thousand at the most.'

'A doublet?' Peter asked.

'You take a diamond,' Ted explained with gestures, 'and cement it carefully onto a glass backing. Voila! You have a doublet, diamond on top and glass underneath. Very hard to tell unless you're an expert.'

'I can see that,' Peter said.

'And then there's the triplet . . . '

'Enough. I'll take you along with me the next time I buy a diamond.'

'Oh, I just know these things exist; I couldn't spot one if someone waved it in my face. Luckily, I have no craving for diamonds.'

'I believe we're going a bit astray,' Professor Perlemutter said from the depths of his chair. 'Prefect Damarat, you don't know of any other potential targets for your criminal guests?'

'No. There's the paper mill, but I think that's a bit far-fetched.'

Smith looked interested. 'The paper mill? I don't know about that.'

'What's of particular value there?' Ted asked. 'Do they have a big payroll?'

'Yes, there's always that, but that wasn't what I was thinking of. The Duchy of Alba paperworks has been producing high-grade paper for the past hundred and fifty years. A good part of its output is used for stock for paper money by several European governments. A large supply of the paper would be invaluable to counterfeiters.'

Smith snapped his fingers. 'That's it! That's the detail I was looking for. Now I think I know what that clever devil is planning.' He started pacing the floor and slapping his fist into his palm. 'When, that's the question; when and how. We have to find out.'

'I'm afraid you've rather left the rest of us behind,' Professor Perlemutter told the thin, pacing figure.

'I will try to explain,' Smith said. 'There is in the world a man — or perhaps, as some think, a devil — who has been responsible for more of the pure evil loosed upon this planet for the last eighty years than any other force. Wherever the tendrils of evil are to be found, the presence of this man may be detected in the shadows.'

'Excuse me,' Peter said. 'Did you say 'eighty years'?'

'I did,' Smith told him. 'I myself have been his nemesis for the past forty years. I have chased him, thwarted his plans, and sometimes almost caught him, but he has always managed to elude me at the last instant. He is fiendishly clever, and utterly ruthless.'

'I grant that,' Peter said. 'But how old is he?'

Smith shrugged. 'You may choose to think I exaggerate when I say eighty years, but I have reason to believe that it may be even longer than that. The man is incredibly old. He is living proof of the folk saying 'Only the good die young.' Forty years ago, when I first met him, I was a young man, newly entered in the Intelligence Service. He was already ancient.'

'Who is this man?' Professor Perlemutter asked.

'His correct name, as best I have been able to determine, is the Marquis Chang Hu. He is said to be in the direct line of descent of the royal family of the Manchu Dynasty, and I have no reason to dispute this.'

'He's Chinese, then,' Ted said.

'He claims no country and no country claims him. I know that he spent many years in a monastery in Tibet known as Bache Churan.' Smith stopped and looked around him. After a few seconds, he continued deliberately, 'The monastery produced many wise men whose unique powers are still spoken of in that part of the world. Most of them were good men and worked to help mankind. Some were not. I also know that Bache Churan burned to the ground and was totally destroyed in the year 1906.'

Damarat said, 'But that was over sixty years ago.'

'I am aware of that,' said Smith.

'Tell me,' Professor Perlemutter said, leaning forward, his hands on his knees, 'where do you see the hand of this, ah, evil genius in the events here in Alba?'

'I'm not surprised you find this hard to believe,' Smith said. 'You doubt me.'

'I assure you, sir, I do not find the

presence of evil abroad in the world hard to believe. I have seen too many examples of human actions that can only be described by reference to the concept of evil. I do not doubt you, I merely seek information.'

'You want to know why I see the hand of the Marquis Chang Hu in the events here in Graustark.'

'Yes, sir. You tie the change in attitude of the previously passive spies and the influx of gangsters together, and say that the common element in this mix is your old, ah, opponent the Marquis. How do you know?'

Smith started pacing the floor, with his hands firmly linked behind his back. 'There are signs,' he said. 'If you know what to look for, there are signs. A wave of unrest in an otherwise peaceful place. A mysterious disappearance. An unexplainable murder. A pattern of many elements, seemingly disconnected, which can be made whole only by assuming the presence of a central malevolent figure. If you look, you will find him there: in the center of a web of evil. The slightest touch anywhere on the web will be enough to reveal his loathsome presence. This is the Marquis Chang Hu, last of the Manchu princes.'

Peter looked at Professor Perlemutter, who, he found, was staring at him. Smith no longer seemed quite sane. He was as a man in the grip of a magnificent obsession. His eyes gleamed as he paced the floor, and his hands twisted nervously behind him.

'You, ah, spoke of a mysterious disappearance,' Perlemutter said. 'Did someone disappear?'

'That was what brought me here. One of my agents, a man named Petrie, the son of an old friend, was here on assignment. His report gave the barest suggestion that something might be happening in Alba. Then he disappeared. That was two months ago.'

'You think this man Chang has him?'

'If Chang had him two months ago, then he is most assuredly dead by now.'

Damarat laughed. 'Come, come, Smith. Don't you think this is all a bit melodramatic? A mysterious evil genius who kills like *that* — ' He snapped his fingers. ' — without compunction or fear of consequences? I'm not saying the man doesn't exist; but surely no one can be as capable or as bad as you paint this fellow.'

Smith drew himself up. His whole bearing had a powerful, compelling quality. 'I am witness,' he said, 'to this man's past. I tell you, sir, that I do not exaggerate. If he thinks any of us stand in his way, he would kill us with less compunction than you uproot a radish. He has sworn to kill me. He has almost — '

There was a crash, and a section of the window burst inward. Shards of glass flew all over the room. A loud hiss blotted out all other sound as a metal cylinder bounced off the far wall and onto the floor. Thick white smoke sprayed out in all directions, and the cylinder jerked and spun around with a life of its own.

'Hold your breath!' Smith shouted, and dived after the cylinder. It spun by him, and Peter, without pausing to think, grabbed it and flung it out the window in one motion. Professor Perlemutter, showing surprising agility for one of his girth, had leaped to the door the second he saw the smoke. 'Outside, quick,' he said, holding the door open. Peter helped Smith to his feet, and they stumbled out after the others.

'Quick thinking,' Smith said when the door was safely closed and they could breathe again.

Damarat looked shaken. 'What was it?' he asked.

'By the slight whiff I got, I'd say cyanide gas,' Professor Perlemutter said. 'Is everyone all right?'

'I burned my hand,' Peter said, examining the injured fingers. 'Those gas grenades generate a lot of heat.'

'We'll get some salve for it,' Damarat said.

'Good,' Peter agreed. 'But first let me run cold water over it for a few minutes; that's the best way to prevent blisters from forming.'

'Who could have done that?' Damarat wondered. 'And why?'

'Another question is — how?' Ted observed. 'We're seven floors up, and there aren't any buildings around here higher than two stories.' Peter looked at Smith. 'Do you think it's the work of your Chinese friend?'

'It has his mark,' Smith said. 'A deadly blow, delivered without warning and when you least expect it. I'd say we'd all best be on our toes from now on.'

5

The man known as Mickey looked around him at the assembled men who were waiting for him to speak. 'The traditions are being observed,' he said, waving a pudgy hand at the surroundings. 'Notice: a dank cellar, a secret passage, a codeword, cover names — the whole rigmarole. I'm a great believer in tradition.'

A short, swarthy man at the far end of the table shifted nervously in his seat as a drop of water fell from the vaulted stone ceiling with a slight plopping sound. Two seconds later, another drop fell, adding to the growing damp spot on the table in front of him. 'Cut the crap, Lasky. Why are we here?'

'Mickey,' the man said. 'Remember that. If you can't remember that, point to whoever you want to talk to. Most of us here know each other; these precautions are being taken for a valid reason which I shall explain. I am Mickey. The gentleman to my right is Donald. You are Goofy. The name, I hasten to assure you, was chosen from the list at random, like all the others. Please do not make that mistake again.'

A thin man in evening dress, with the carefully cultured good looks of a professional gigolo, raised his hand from his position to Mickey's left.

Mickey nodded. 'Yes, Prince Valiant, what is it?'

'I think you've gone slightly overboard on these comic book names,' he said in a cultured voice, his English carrying the overtones of an unidentifiable middle-European accent. 'But that is not my concern. I think that, ah, Goofy, has a valid point. I abandoned a profitable venture to come here on your assurance that it would be — if I remember your exact phrase — more than worthwhile. As far as setting goes, I would personally rather be discussing this at Donnaloni's over a good dinner and a bottle of wine. But as long as I'm here, I'd like to know why.'

'But naturally,' Mickey said smoothly. 'I will be as brief as possible, but you'll have to bear with me for a moment. I have a proposition to put forth that I sincerely hope will interest all of you. After hearing it you are perfectly free to adjourn — separately, of course — to Donnaloni's to enjoy the finest they have to offer, secure in the knowledge that you'll be able to afford the best far into the future.' It obviously sounded good to the men around the table. Some of them leaned forward to hear better, some leaned back, relaxed, some just stopped fidgeting; but they all looked expectant.

'I hope I shan't disappoint any of you,' Mickey said. 'Here's the proposition:

'You are all freelance agents, the best in Europe. Some of you work for one client, some for another. Most of you have worked, at various times, for several clients. Your pay has been commensurate with your abilities. Sometimes it's a salary for the duration of the job, sometimes on a piecework basis. It is, as I have reason to know, not a way to get rich.' Mickey waved a fat hand in the air. 'Oh, I'll admit that, with a bit of luck, a man can do quite well in this business. Some individual properties have had quite a high market value. But, nonetheless, this is not a way to get rich.'

A thickset man halfway down the table leaned forward. 'Look, Mickey Mouse,' he growled, 'save the market analysis. Let's get down to the nitty-gritty.'

'What?' Mickey asked, looking slightly startled.

'What our learned colleague, um, Dick Tracy, is trying to express,' Prince Valiant said, 'is a desire for you to come to the heart of the matter.'

'And I had thought myself fairly colloquial,' Mickey sighed. 'Oh, well . . . The 'nitty-gritty' is this: I am offering you a chance to get rich. So rich that you can each spend the rest of your life living off the bank interest of the principal this little venture will provide.'

A small, dapper man, with a thin-line mustache, raised a well-manicured hand. He was dressed like a British banker, down to the umbrella folded at his feet and the bowler hat placed neatly on the table in front of him.

'Yes, Albert?'

Albert dropped his hand back into his lap. 'As you have observed,' he said in a clipped voice, 'we are all here freelance agents. That would indicate that over the years we have all demonstrated an aversion to working in any formal organization for any length of time. It sounds as if you are proposing an organization, and a contract that will require some time to complete. If so, I, at least, am not interested.'

'I think you should hear me out,' Mickey said patiently. 'I am, indeed, proposing an organization. But not in the usual sense. You might say I am suggesting that we form a union. In a sense we are going to strike for higher wages. The strike should last three weeks, and the settlement will be immediate. A month from now, the organization will be disbanded and we shall all be rich. Are you interested?'

'Go on,' Albert said.

'Yes. Gentlemen, there is a job here in the Grand Duchy of Alba that I am suggesting we take on. It is, in the usual sense of the word, a criminal operation. But it is one which no criminals could take on, because they lack the requisite skills. Those skills are assembled around this table.'

Prince Valiant laughed. 'You're not suggesting that we should knock over the casino, are you? I suppose it would be one way of getting some of my money back.'

'You're out of your skull,' the thickset Dick Tracy said, standing up. 'The most we could get from the casino would be five million dollars. After fencing it, that's about two and a half million. You've got thirty people in here; that's about eighty thousand apiece. It's not worth the risk. Count me out.'

'Sit down!' Mickey snapped.

'Don't open your yap to me,' the heavy man said. 'If I want to walk out, I walk out.'

'I'm sorry,' Mickey said smoothly. 'I apologize for yelling. It's a bad trait that I should keep under control. I am not going to suggest that we — as you put it — 'knock over' the casino. Please sit down and hear me out.'

'Okay,' Tracy said, dropping back into his chair. 'I'll listen, but talk civil to me.'

'I do apologize. It was not only impolite of me: it was bad management. I admit to an error.' Mickey sounded displeased with himself. 'It won't happen again, I make few mistakes, and I never repeat them.'

He took a deep breath and continued. 'It is, as I've said, essentially a criminal operation, not something we would usually consider. But I think in this case the gain is worth both the risk and the uniqueness of the job. We are indeed going to 'knock over' something, but not the casino. Something far more valuable to us.' He paused and looked around, waiting for comment, but he was holding his audience.

'We are going to rob the Royal Alban Paperworks.'

'A paper mill?' someone snorted.

'What the hell,' someone else said.

'You're kidding,' Prince Valiant laughed again. 'Where's the profit?'

'Gentlemen,' Mickey said. He slapped the table. 'Gentlemen!'

The murmur stopped, and he regained his audience. 'I assure you that I am not crazy. Does anyone know what the principal product of the Royal Alban Paperworks is?'

'Paper,' Dick Tracy said, starting to get up again. 'Don't tell me you're not crazy.'

'Wait a minute,' Prince Valiant said. 'Wait just a minute. Now I remember. Paper indeed, but of a very special sort.'

Dick Tracy paused halfway out of his chair. The pose made him look like a squatting gorilla in a sport jacket. 'What's so special about paper?'

'This paper is money,' Prince Valiant told him.

'Money?' Dick Tracy sat back down.

'That is correct,' Mickey said. 'This paper is at least halfway to being money. It is the special stock that twelve different countries use to print their currency on. It's carefully controlled, and almost impossible to duplicate.'

'How does that make it valuable to us?' Dick Tracy asked, sounding interested. 'Are we going into the counterfeiting business?'

'Not at all,' Mickey assured him. 'The paper is shipped in one-meter-square sheets. I have a client that will pay us slightly under a hundred dollars a sheet.'

'How many sheets?' Prince Valiant asked.

'There is a shipment of five hundred thousand sheets being prepared. That is what I propose to acquire.'

'That's fifty million dollars,' Dick Tracy said. He was firmly rooted to his chair.

'That is correct. There are twenty-seven of us. Even shares, after subtracting collection costs and my, er, finder's fee, will come to close to two million dollars, American, apiece. Certainly enough to retire on.'

'Five hundred thousand sheets of paper must take up a lot of room,' someone commented.

'About fifty-six cubic meters,' Mickey said. 'It's all figured out.'

'Go ahead,' Dick Tracy said. 'Let's hear the figuring.'

'Before I continue, is everyone here interested in my proposition? I'd rather not give out any more data if anyone is planning to leave this little gathering without accepting my offer of employment. This is the time to speak up, gentlemen. Are there any questions aside from the details of the operation?'

'How immediate is payment?' someone asked.

'Within a week. Guaranteed.'

'Who is your client?'

'I am not at liberty to disclose that. Take my word that the interested party is willing and able to pay the agreed sum upon completion of the assignment. The consumer has a triple-A rating throughout our business. Some of you have worked for this client before.'

'A government?' one of them asked.

Mickey frowned. 'Let us just say that it is an organization that's quite able to pay the fee. Donald here is aware of their identity, and I think he'll bear me out.'

John Kott nodded. 'That's right,' he said flatly, speaking for the first time.

'What currency will we be paid in?'

'United States dollars. All bills in denominations of a hundred or smaller. Quite untraceable.' Mickey smiled. 'None counterfeit.'

The short man known as Goofy stood up nervously. 'This operation,' he asked.

'It will require violence?'

'That is evident,' Mickey agreed. 'But I am aware that some of us are, let us say, constitutionally averse to violence. There will be several jobs that will be quite nonviolent. I have you slated for one of those.' There was the suggestion of a sneer in his voice.

'It still sounds dangerous. Physical violence makes me sick. I don't think I'm interested.'

'Bah!' someone snorted. 'You're noted for knifing people in the back. It's just facing them that upsets you.'

'Are you sure?' Mickey asked. 'Are you quite positive? I'll give you a moment to reconsider. Don't you agree that the gain is worth the risk?'

'Yes. Of course. I just don't think I'm up to the risk. Every man should be aware of his own limitations, and that's mine. Does the offer of a thousand francs for listening to your proposition still hold?'

'Naturally. I never go back on my word. You're entitled to something for my having taken up your time. Are you sure you're out?'

'Yes.'

'Fine.' Mickey looked around. 'Is there anyone else? Are you all quite sure? Very good. Donald, would you take this gentleman to the other room and pay him off. As soon as he's gone we can continue.' Kott stood up and walked toward the back room. The short man trotted after him.

As soon as they had left, a wave of conversation broke out around the table. Mickey ignored it and just stood silently, waiting.

The sound of a pistol shot blasted out of the back room and reverberated around the thick stone walls. A sharp, heavy noise, close to the pain level in the enclosed room, it blotted out all other sound. When it died down the conversation had ceased.

John Kott walked slowly back into the room and took his seat. Mickey leaned over the table and smiled. 'I think we can continue now,' he said.

6

Peter sat with his eyes closed and his feet up on the battered desk in the tiny office he'd been given, and allowed his mind to wander. It was the position he found most conducive to creative thinking. He tried not to let any of his coworkers catch him that way, because they always assumed he was asleep and that was bad for morale, but this morning he was alone for a while.

There were several elements in the present situation that needed sorting out. Ted Ursa was downstairs, going over lists of police equipment to establish what needed modernizing. Professor Perlemutter was in with Damarat, going over the qualifications of various candidates for the head of the to-be-formed counter-intelligence section. That left Peter alone to do the sorting.

Since the gas attack two days ago, several things had happened. They had established, on the word of a policeman who had seen the event and chased the culprit two blocks before losing him, that the cyanide cylinder had been lofted through the window by a crossbow. The monomaniacal Mister Smith had gone off like a man possessed and disappeared, promising to reappear with whatever information he could gather. The body of an innocuous, low-level spy, who regularly wintered in Alba, was found folded in half and stuck in the garbage can behind a cheap restaurant, with a bullet through his head. Interpol forwarded the dossiers of several more criminal types who were believed to be in, or headed toward, the Grand Duchy of Alba. Something, Peter felt idiotically sure, was happening or going to happen in Alba. The question remained: What was the nature of the happening?

The more Peter thought about the events of the past few days, the more convinced he became that Mister Smith was at least partly right. Whether the omnipotent and diabolical Marquis Chang Hu was really involved, or whether Smith, whatever the game, saw the Marquis as the player on the other side, was a moot point. Peter now believed that Smith had been correct in assuming that all the recent events in Alba were somehow connected. As an old army dictum had it: Once is happenstance, twice is coincidence, three times is enemy action. Now that the existence of a specific enemy had been postulated, all that remained was to establish his identity and his goal.

Peter lit a cigarette and blew smoke thoughtfully at the ceiling. *All that remains!* he thought. *Hellfire and damnation. Now that I know I'm playing blindfold chess, all I have to do is find out how many moves my opponent has made and where my king is.*

'Aha! Sound asleep as usual,' Professor Perlemutter boomed from the doorway. 'Well, no matter. I shall tippy-toe about the room and not disturb you.' He stomped into the office.

Peter shifted his feet off the desk and sat up. 'Tippy-toe more quietly, please. You interrupt a deep contemplation.'

'Thinking about the meaning of creation, no doubt,' Perlemutter said, looking at a calendar posted across the room which bore the usual nude picture of an impossibly proportioned young lady. 'I believe the type of thoughts resulting from staring at that picture could be termed thinking about creation.' He eased himself into a chair.

'That's enough of your heavy-handed Teutonic humor. What's your problem?'

'I have in my hand,' Professor Perlemutter said, displaying his hand, 'the deciphered text of the last message turned over by that boy Marko before the spies got him. It was just received from our computer section back in New Jersey.'

'Fast work,' Peter commented. 'We only sent it to them two days ago. Those boys are sharp.'

'Sharper than you think. Bob Alvin didn't break the code, he recognized it.'

'How's that?'

'Here's the text,' Perlemutter said, handing Peter the teletype carbon. 'It's probably the most famous message in the world to cryptographers.'

The message read:

AUSWARTIGES AMT TELE-GRAPHIERT JANUAR 16 COLON

NUMBER 1 GANZ GEHEIM SELBST ZU ENTZIFFERN STOP WIR BEABSICHTIGEN AM ERSTEN PEBRUAR UNEINGESCHRANKT U-BOOT KRIEG ZU BEGINNEN STOP ES WIRD VERSUCHT WERDEN VEREINIGTEN STAATEN TROTZDEM NEUTRAL ZU ERHALTEN STOP

'German?' Peter queried, reading the carbon. His glance fastened on one phrase. 'What's this about unrestricted submarine warfare? Sounds like something from World War I.'

'Indeed it does,' Perlemutter agreed. 'You are now looking at the opening paragraphs of the world famous Zimmermann telegram.'

'The Zimmermann . . . ? Oh yes, the message from the Kaiser's Foreign Minister to the President of Mexico, asking him to declare war on the United States.'

'That's the one. It was intercepted and decrypted in 1917 by the British, who turned the text over to the American government. Its publication in American newspapers raised quite a stink and helped bring the United States into the war.'

'Quite a document,' Peter said. 'What's it doing here today?'

'My question exactly,' Perlemutter agreed. He rested his chin on his hands and stared at the top of the desk. 'I think our adversary has a sense of humor; and I've always maintained that there's nothing in the world as dangerous as a villain with a sense of humor.'

Peter pulled a long, dark cigar out of his breast pocket, carefully nipped the end off it, and applied the flame from a gold lighter to the other end. He puffed thoughtfully toward the ceiling for a long moment. 'I suppose we don't have any of the originals of our various intercepted messages?'

'I am forced to concede that you suppose correctly,' Perlemutter said, sniffing the air. 'A Van Groot?'

Peter extracted a second cigar from the pocket and tossed it to Professor Perlemutter. 'If we don't have the original documents, we can't very well test them for secret inks or microdots, can we?'

'I suppose,' Professor Perlemutter said, rolling the cigar between his palms, 'that what we must do is pray for a new missive.'

'Have we any other agents in the enemy camp?' Peter asked.

Professor Perlemutter planted the cigar firmly between his teeth and pulled a large wooden match out of his pocket. Glaring at Peter, he lit the match with his thumbnail and the cigar with the match. Then he blew the match out and carefully placed it in the large ashtray on the desk. 'No,' he said.

'Then you really must believe in the power of prayer,' Peter commented.

'Well,' Perlemutter said, blowing clouds toward the far wall, 'as the student said to the barmaid; it's all I've got.'

'Then we must look for something else.'

'That's what she said,' Perlemutter agreed.

'Have you and Signore Damarat agreed on the basics for Alba's CIC?'

'We have. Damarat has picked a bright

young detective first grade to head it. Name's Loupe.'

'What's the cover name for the section?'

'We decided to ride right out in the open. It's called Section Seven — Security.'

'A good, honest sound, that,' Peter said. 'No beating around the bush. Now our only problem is finding out what Section Seven has to secure.'

Professor Perlemutter nodded his agreement from the middle of a cloud of burning Van Groot.

7

Hong pi-Hing sat quietly in his seat, fingering his copy of *The Thoughts of Chairman Mao* and looking out the airplane window at the flat white blanket that covered the world below. Being a man who had long ago learned to take contentment in the small doses in which it was offered, he was content. The Comrade Stewardess had paused in her leading of a group reading of selected passages in *The Thoughts*, advised silent study and meditation on the great words, and gone off to make tea. The pause couldn't last long — how long does it take to make tea? — but Hong was grateful for the brief sanity of silence.

Hong had often thought that he was born a hundred years out of his time. A hundred years ago he could have led a full and quiet life as an official of the Manchu court. A hundred years from now, for that matter, when the New China had settled down, he could again be a quiet, efficient bureaucrat. It was the interim time of this new dynasty that called itself the People's Republic, with its new rulers that called themselves Communists, that was upsetting to live in. It was a time in which children not only disobeyed their parents but beat up their teachers, and all in the name of the people. Hong's father would have been shocked.

The Comrade Stewardess, with a large tray of tea glasses in her beefy hands, marched back into the passenger compartment and started passing out the glasses. Hong smiled up at the solidly-built girl and took his tea. The problem now was to find a way to avoid going back to chanting the dull, contradictory passages from China's new red-jacketed bible.

Hong decided to subtly pull rank. If he were to bluntly tell the girl that, as an official of the Ministry of Outcountry Cultural Affairs, he outranked her, she would merely tell him that, in that case, it would be his privilege to lead the chanting. Just what he wanted to avoid.

He opened his ancient briefcase and pulled out a folder that was conspicuously stamped with the ministry seal. Carefully placing it seal-up, he withdrew the papers it contained and bent over them: the picture of a dedicated official who would even give up the privilege of chanting *The Thoughts of Chairman Mao* to keep up with his important work.

The stewardess finished her tea-time chore and stationed herself in the middle of the aisle with the red-covered book clutched firmly to her ample breasts. 'Comrades,' she boomed, 'we were reading from page seventeen. I will continue.'

Hong looked up, smiled, and nodded his approval, then went back to his important papers. The look the girl flashed at him was indecipherable, but she led the rest of the passengers in the uplifting reading without bothering Hong.

To shut out the drone of voices surrounding him, Hong did his best to concentrate on the few, almost-memorized, papers before him. Most of them were just rather inane directives as to the best way to conduct his job in Albania: that of bringing the small European country even more firmly into an orbit which centered on the People's Republic of China. One of the directives, which Hong regarded with the special favor a parent reserves for an imbecile child, told him to stress the racial similarity between the Chinese and the Albanians. 'What,' Hong wondered mildly, 'racial similarity?' There were the Mongol hordes that swept through both Europe and Asia in the fourteenth century. Through a strange chance series of rapes, a Chinese and an Albanian could be cousins — five hundred years removed.

Hong looked casually around him to make sure none of his near plane-mates were taking an undue interest in his affairs. They all seemed to be absorbed in the wisdom of Chairman Mao. Hong put his seat up to further isolate himself from his companions, and set his papers flat down on the small table that pulled out of the seat in front of him. He was now reasonably sure that nobody could accidentally read over or around his shoulder. These elementary precautions taken to satisfy his conscience, Hong now pulled out of the folder the two rice paper pages that dealt with the second, and more interesting, half of his job.

The Ministry of Outcountry Cultural Affairs had the responsibility for certain types of minor intelligence activities, and Hong was glad to include these activities among his jobs when he went Outcountry for the M. of O.C.A. This minor spying had several advantages for Hong. It raised his pay but, because of the secret fetish of all intelligence work, conveyed no increase in status. Hong wasn't interested in status, feeling that the chicken that stuck his neck above the flock was the first to get the axe. It also gave him a handle to open the door to asylum if Hong ever thought it necessary to defect. First, it gave him access to the ways of getting out of his country; and second, it gave him knowledge of potential interest to the country he would defect to. Hong was a great believer in the tit-for-tat principle, and kept his supply of tat on hand.

The current problem, as outlined by the two pages of neatly-written ideograms, promised to be fascinating. In the latest monthly communication from the Albanian People's Secret Police, they mentioned the culmination of preparations for Operation Smash and Grab, and thanked the M. of O.C.A. for its assistance. Internal evidence in the communication indicated that this had something to do with the Grand Duchy of Alba, Albania's northern neighbor.

What made this an interesting problem was that the M. of O.C.A. knew nothing about Operation Smash and Grab. Carefully worded questions to the rival intelligence organizations in the People's Republic showed that they didn't know any more about it than the Ministry. This opened several unpleasant possibilities. Hong's job was to find out what Operation Smash and Grab was and who had given the Albanian People's Secret Police the assistance they were thanking the M. of O.C.A. for.

The Fasten Seat Belts sign went on, and the pilot announced the approach to Zagreb. Hong put the papers back in his briefcase and settled back in his seat. This promised to be an interesting mission.

In the ancient monastery of St. Simon, perched on a crag in the lofty reaches of the Dinaric Alps in northern Albania, brown-clad monks scurried about in the order's perpetual imitation of a colony of eager ants. The order was closed to outsiders, so there was no one to tell that these brown-robed and hooded men were not the same as the peaceful winemakers who had occupied the monastery in unbroken succession from the founding of the order to a scant two years before. These men were new, and how they got to the monastery and what happened to those who were here when they arrived was not recorded in the order's large and massive daybook. It could, perhaps, be deduced if one were to accidentally uncover the large filled-in pit just outside the ancient walls and find therein the bodies of some three hundred elderly men and a few youngsters. Some had crushed skulls; some had severed necks; a few had one or more bullets in the chest cavity; most seemed to have died in a paroxysm of agony, such as is induced by the breathing of certain virulent gases. All had met unnatural ends, insofar as a death can ever said to be unnatural.

The monastery was dominated by a large central chamber that had been, over a period of centuries, hollowed out of the side of the mountain against which the outer buildings huddled, and was surrounded by a wide gallery. During the period when the monastery was inhabited by those who belonged to it, the chamber was used for prayer and tribute to the glory of God. Now it was filled with large, square, boxy machines that chuckled to themselves, and a host of brown-clad men that ministered to their needs.

On the gallery overlooking the central chamber, an individual in the brown robe of a monk, hooded and edged with gold thread, paced restlessly back and forth across the sandstone-paved floor, his tall figure casting weird shadows in the chamber below as it intersected the rays of the sodium vapor lamps newly installed in the vaulted rock ceiling high above.

A squat man in plain brown robes

stood by the door of the gallery. 'The day's reports, milord.'

'Good, good,' the tall one said. 'Hand them here.' He took the pleated pages of computer print-out and resumed his pacing as he read:

**16929 Branch Group A on schedule. Branch
16930 Group B on schedule. All ready to
16931 proceed with combined operation,
16932 Branch Group**

'Excellent. In regard to action groups A and B, tell them to go on as planned. The final date will be communicated to them within the week.'

The squat man made a notation in a small notebook.

**16945 ation of celerity. I scan. I scan. Ap
16946 pearance of agents of Weapons An
16947 alysis and
16948 Research Corporation in Alba at
16949 present
16950 must be considered suspicious.
16951 Prob: 19/489.3 Albert.**

'In regard to these men of War, Incorporated who have so suddenly shown up in Alba: we cannot assume that they know nothing and just appeared at this time by a fortuitous accident. Therefore, we must find out what they do know. Have their leader — this Carthage — kidnapped and brought here.'

The squat man nodded and made another notation.

16989 lately. The appearance of Smith, or
16990 possibly many Smiths, cannot be
16991 overlooked. Smith must be de
16992 stroyed. Smith must

'Have you noticed that this machine seems to be paranoid on the subject of Smith? It must be something in its programming, I'll have to look into it.'

'Yes, milord. What should we do about Smith?'

'Ah, well. I have no further time for these games. Do we have him located?'

'Our agent lost contact with him four days ago.'

'Why wasn't I told? Why — ' He shook

the paper. ' — wasn't the machine told?'

'The information was fed into the machine, just as all other information as processed. The machine seems to have some sort of block on the subject. It insists in calling every British agent a 'Smith,' and therefore has a hard time keeping track of the real one.'

'I'll have to have that looked into,' the tall man promised. 'Now, about the, er, real Smith — find him and kill him.'

'Very good, milord.'

17000 scan. I scan. Break. Attention, in
17001 vestigator by name Hong pi-Hing ar
17002 riving P.R. of Albania from P.R. of
17003 China 16/14/2330 on flight 23. Must
17004 be removed before he communicates
17005 with P.R. of Albania authorities.
17006 Must be interrogated.

'This Hong pi-Hing. You will have him taken care of?'

'It is arranged.'

'Do not allow him to communicate with anyone until he arrives here.'

'It shall be as you say.' The tall man nodded and waved the squat man away.

*   *   *

Hong pi-Hing deplaned down the ancient, rusty loading ramp, clutching his briefcase to his side. He nodded to the pudgy stewardess, who was wearing the smug smile of one who has done a stupid job well. *She looks*, he reflected as he passed her, *like a cow in heat. She must have a bull nearby. I hope he's fond of the words of Chairman Mao, whoever he is.*

Hong and his fellow passengers followed a dour-faced Albanian customs official into a large tin shed. Inside the shed, the official gathered them all together under the glare of one of the unshielded bulbs that hung from the ceiling, and called off a list of names from the passenger manifest. Everyone answered.

The official waggled his mustache. 'Very good,' he said. 'Wait here.' He walked away.

An elderly man standing next to Hong asked, 'What did he say?'

'You don't speak Albanian?' Hong asked.

'No.'

'He asked us to wait here.'

'Oh.' The man nodded. 'What for?'

'He didn't say. For our luggage, I would assume.'

'Oh. Is that man waving to you?' Hong looked over to the other side of the customs barrier. There was a young man in the semi-official uniform of the Chinese Government, black pants and mattress-ticking jacket, who seemed to be waving at him. 'That's funny,' Hong said, 'I didn't expect to be met.'

'The unexpected,' the oldster told him, 'is the spice in the sauce of life.'

'Lao-tzu?' Hong asked.

The old man shrugged. 'If Chairman Mao hasn't said it, I'm sure he will.'

Hong decided to have not heard that, and nodded politely to the old man before walking over to the barrier.

'You are Comrade Hong pi-Hing?' the youth on the far side of the barrier asked when Hong had approached to within conversational speaking distance.

'I am. I wasn't aware that anyone was to meet me.'

The young man looked disinterested. 'I was just going to tell you that we've expedited your passage through Customs and you can come with me now; but if you'd prefer to wait, I'll leave and meet you later at the Embassy.'

'I meant no offense,' Hong said hastily, looking back at the confused throng of fellow passengers. 'I assure you I'm quite grateful to you for having taken the trouble.'

'Come along then,' the young man said. He indicated a gate further down the fence. 'You can go through there.'

Hong walked rapidly around and rejoined the young man. 'What about my luggage?' he asked.

'We'll see to it. It'll be along presently.'

'Fine,' Hong said.

As the youth steered Hong toward the parking area his car was in, Hong marveled at the service. Up till now, he had been convinced that even the Ambassador must carry his own luggage and take the local bus to the Embassy. The People of the people's republics seemed to think that doing anything for anyone else was degrading.

The youth led a contented Hong over to a middle-aged, respectable black car in the lot, and Hong climbed into the back. It wasn't until he was inside that he realized that there was someone else in there with him.

'Hello,' the someone else said pleasantly. Something suddenly went *thunk* against the side of Hong's head, and Hong collapsed against the back of the seat.

'That's that,' the man said. 'I hope he doesn't bleed on the upholstery.'

8

Ted Ursa, resplendent in summer dinner jacket, bow tie and massive gold cufflinks, was sprawled over a chair in the hotel lobby reading a paperback when Peter and Professor Perlemutter stepped out of the elevator. He waved the book in greeting. 'What's been keeping you? I've almost finished the first page already.'

'The first page?' Peter laughed. 'I'm not impressed.'

'You should be,' Ted told him. 'It's in Italian, and I don't read Italian.' He put the book down. 'How do I look?'

Peter examined him critically. 'You look as if your only problem is deciding which stock to buy with this month's dividends.'

The WAR, Inc. crew crossed the lobby of the Excelsior and went down the wide, marble steps to the piazza. Across the square, on top of a squat white building, rows of large round lightbulbs spelled out the word CASINO. They walked leisurely toward the building.

'How much are you going to lose tonight?' Peter asked.

'I have twenty-five dollars, with which I'm prepared to teach the Italians who run this place how to shoot craps,' Ted said.

'I plan to risk about twenty-five myself,' Peter said. He turned to Professor Perlemutter. 'How about you?'

'I have not established an upper limit,' the Professor said. 'I have a system. It was developed by my maternal grandfather.'

At the great doors of the casino, a blue-coated lackey collected the courtesy cards the hotel had given them — to introduce them, verify their credit, and eliminate the need for them to pay a fee upon entering — and escorted them into the great central room. 'Through there,' he said, indicating an open door at the far end of the room, 'is the open baccarat table. The doors to the side lead to rooms for private games.' He pointed to a wide staircase in the entrance hall behind them. 'Upstairs is the nightclub.'

'The nightclub?' Perlemutter asked.

The man nodded. 'It is called the Club Casino d'Alba. Dining and dancing for those who desire. Enjoy yourselves, gentlemen.' He bowed slightly and left.

'Well,' Ted said, rubbing his hands together, 'I believe that green-covered table over there must be the place set aside for the noble sport of rolling the bones. It looks a little different from the back alleys of Atlanta.'

'Think you'll adjust?' Peter asked.

'I'll do my best.' He wandered off toward the table in question.

Professor Perlemutter surveyed the room. 'What's your pleasure, Colonel Carthage?'

Peter said, 'I don't know, Professor. I think I'll just spend some time looking around. The people here interest me as much as the play.'

'Well, enjoy yourself, my boy. I perceive that there is a *chemin de fer* table that looks like it could use the instructive support of my grandfather's system. I think I'll go over and introduce myself into the game.'

'Have fun. I'll come over later and bail

you out, if you're not in too deep by then.'

⋆ ⋆ ⋆

Peter roamed around the great main room of the two-hundred-year-old Casino d'Alba, examining the luxurious decor and watching the elegant patrons. The three elaborate cut-glass chandeliers, famous landmarks of the casino, each supporting more than fifteen tons of glass and wire, blossomed from the vaulted roof of the casino main room and cast the subdued twinkle of gaslight around the room. The lights in the wall fixtures around the room were electric, but dimmer than the gas.

The atmosphere of the gambling casino was that of dreamland, and bright lights might drive away the dreams. At one time, the titled and wealthy of Europe might have frequented this and other old-world, wood-paneled, thick-carpeted cathedrals of card and chip; but these days, for every countess there were five shopgirls, and for each millionaire there

118

were ten to a hundred shoe salesmen and insurance clerks.

This happened to be what those in the know called the 'season,' and the leavening of people that browsed among the gambleware in the great hall were, indeed, mostly wealthy and titled. But in a mere two weeks, vacation time would come for millions of the ordinary; the well-dressed, quiet gentlemen and ladies who now stood at the tables and wagered with the large, rectangular chips would fade away, to be replaced by the baggy shorts and print shirts of the hordes who would surround the tables three-deep and shout and giggle as they bet one or two of the small, round chips. The casino would put a turnstile at the front door, take some of the older paintings off the wall, and charge three lire admission — please check your flash equipment if you have a camera.

A soft voice behind Peter said distinctly 'One of these round, white things that says *Societe Anonyme du Casino du Grand Duchy d'Alba* around the edge for your thoughts.'

Peter turned. Standing next to him was a beautiful woman. Around her, softly clinging, supporting, and revealing, was the gown Cinderella might have worn to the ball if the story had been written for adults. The heat of her body caused to evaporate and waft across to Peter a delicate scent the finest perfumers of Paris had spent years in perfecting so that, combined with a woman, it would create desire. It did.

Peter bowed slightly, feeling that this was the only appropriate gesture. 'Good evening, Miss Blaire. I must say, it's a pleasure to see you again.'

'You must?' Maggi asked.

Peter nodded, smiling. 'It's a compulsion.'

'I'm glad of that. It's a welcome compulsion that makes you want to see me again. Nonetheless — ' She held out a small white chip. ' — I'm paying for your thoughts.'

Peter accepted the chip and put it in his pocket. 'A premium price. I thank you. Where are your girls?'

'In bed, I hope. Don't you realize that it's after eleven?'

'After eleven, of course.' Peter laughed.

'How do they take to being put to bed at eleven?'

'By the time I finish working them for the day, they're quite ready to go to sleep. Besides, if I let them find adventure or romance, their parents would have my head.'

'Quite a responsibility.'

Maggi nodded. 'Sometimes I feel more like a housemother than a choreographer. It's gotten so bad that when I go out like this, even though the girls are asleep, I feel guilty.'

'That's bad,' Peter agreed. 'We should do something about it.' He looked around. 'Would you like to, ah, wager your all on a spin of the wheel or a flip of the card?'

'My all? I don't think I'm quite prepared to risk my all quite yet, thank you. I might go so far as to lose this white chip, last of a vanishing hoard.'

They walked over to the nearby roulette table. 'I, as it happens, also have one chip. Why don't we put them together as an investment in our future?'

'An excellent idea,' Maggi agreed. They stood at the foot of the table.

At the head of the table, by the wheel, the croupier was getting ready to give it another spin. '*Faites vos jeux, messieurs et mesdames, Faites vos jeux . . .*'

'Well,' Maggi asked, 'on what should we *fait* our collection of *jeux*?'

Peter stared down at the board. 'We'll put it all on a number.'

'That's what I like,' Maggi said, 'a decisive man. I've always been partial to the number five. What about you?'

'Not that I believe in luck,' Peter said, 'but I kind of like the number seven.'

'Fine,' Maggi said. 'Let's split the difference.'

'Fair enough,' Peter agreed. They each put their chip down on the six.

'*Faites vos jeux,*' the croupier chanted for one last time, and then shoved the big wheel into motion. 'Betting closed.' With an expert flip of his wrist, the croupier sent the little white ball spinning in its groove in the wheel.

Everyone around the table — big bets, small bets, even the impartial croupier — held their breath while the white ball chased itself around the rotating wheel, each spinning in the opposite direction. The wheel slowed down until the numbers could be made out, and then further to a crawl. The ball hopped out of its groove and, for a few heart-stopping seconds, clattered and jumped among the numbers.

'Twelve, red and even,' the croupier announced when the ball stopped jumping. 'Twelve, red and even.' He looked smug, as though he could have told you all the time, if you'd only thought to ask him.

'We've lost,' Peter said. He turned away from the table and looked down sadly. 'I'll have to sell the ranch.'

Maggi squeezed his arm. 'Never mind. I've never been overly fond of cows, anyhow.'

'You're a good woman, Maggi. Let's go somewhere and celebrate.' He held out his arm, and she took it. 'I understand that there's a nightclub upstairs. We could go and see what secret delights it has to offer.'

'Let's do that,' Maggi said. 'I've been hearing about secret delights all my life; it's about time I saw some.'

They went out the door to the entrance hall and started up the staircase. Along the wall, about four feet apart, a row of portraits stepped up. At the bottom of the stairs, the faces peering out of the frames were resting on bodies garbed in fourteenth-century dress. As the pictures climbed, the dress got more modern, until the last one, near the top, appeared in the stiff collar of the late nineteenth century.

The Club Casino d'Alba was marked by a small sign and a pair of open doors. Beyond the doors, a red velvet rope supported by two gold posts cut off their further entrance.

'Hello!' Peter said. 'There doesn't seem to be anyone here.'

'Oh there must be,' Maggi said. 'If the place was closed, the doors wouldn't be opened.'

At that moment the headwaiter appeared from around the corner and hurried toward the rope. 'Ah, Monsieur, Madam, I, Albert, apologize for have keeping you waiting one bit! It is a tragedy. But I am here, and you come in. Yes?' He unhooked the velvet rope and ushered them by. 'Please, after me, and I will have seating you.'

As the headwaiter marched proudly ahead of them, Maggi leaned over and whispered to Peter, 'Where do you think he learned his English?'

'I don't think he ever did,' Peter replied softly.

They rounded the corner and came face to face with the nightclub: a medium-sized, square room with gold carpeting. Except for the bandstand and patch of dance floor, it was liberally sprinkled with tables. The decor was fifty years newer than that in the casino downstairs, which made it fifty years old. The impression it created was a memory of cloche hats and open-air touring cars. On the bandstand, six men were playing a waltz. Aside from these men and the headwaiter, the room was completely deserted.

He ushered them to a table near the bandstand, seated them, and then retreated to the headwaiter-spot by the entrance. A busboy appeared from behind a screen and invested their table with a rose-red tablecloth. A second busboy supplied silverware and large linen napkins. Then the two busboys did a vanishing act, and in their place an immaculate waiter appeared and presented them with two large, stiff cardboard menus.

'We've already eaten,' Peter told the waiter. 'Perhaps a drink?'

'Hrumph,' the waiter said, and left them, to be replaced immediately by a gentleman wearing two large keys.

'A bottle of wine?' Peter asked Maggi.

'That sounds fine,' she agreed.

'Very good, sir. May I suggest a bottle of our Schloss Randall Dachstube?' the wine steward asked earnestly. 'We're quite proud of it.'

'We shall definitely try a bottle, then,' Peter said. The wine steward bowed slightly and left the table.

The wine came, and Maggi tasted it and liked it. 'I admire a man with the courage of his convictions, even in small things,' she said, raising her glass in single toast.

Peter answered the toast. 'I shall always endeavor to prove to be right,' he said.

'Well,' Maggi said. 'Fancy language!'

Peter smiled. 'You seem to bring out the Victorian gentleman in me.'

'Not too Victorian, I hope,' Maggi said

seriously, staring intently into his eyes, as though trying to read some deep message in them.

Peter looked into the depths of this slim, self-assured woman's eyes and saw there, for a second, a lonely little girl looking out. Then the moment of empathy broke, and both of them looked away. 'Would you care to dance?' Peter asked.

'I'd love to,' Maggi told him. They stood up as the band broke into a fresh waltz. Peter put his arm around Maggi's waist, and they floated into a dance from a different world, eighty years in the past.

'I have a feeling,' Maggi said as they whirled about the hardwood dance floor, 'that this room and these people have been sitting here waiting for us since Franz Josef left in 1895.'

The band, perhaps in recognition of this truth, subtly switched from the nondescript tune they were playing to the 'Emperor's Waltz.' Peter thought he recognized the music, then started slightly as he realized what it was. 'Tonight your words seem to create the truth,' he told Maggi. 'Be careful with your wishes.'

Neither of them was sure how long they had danced, but when they did stop they had no energy left. 'I feel like a kid's top,' Peter said. 'As long as I keep whirling around, I'm fine, but when I stop I fall over.' To prove his point he collapsed into his chair.

Maggi sat sedately down next to him, but her eyes were shining. 'No staying power, that's your trouble. Oh my, but wasn't that fun.'

'It was,' Peter agreed. 'I think we move well together.'

Maggi put her hand on Peter's cheek, caressing his ear for a moment, contemplatively, then reached forward and kissed him. 'We might discuss that sometime soon,' she whispered.

Peter smiled and held her hand. 'I'll have to work on my staying power.'

'My goodness,' Maggi said, examining her watch. 'Look what time it is. I really must get back to the hotel and get some sleep. We have a long day tomorrow; the Gala's only four days from now.'

Peter distributed the last of the wine. 'Come, drink up your share and then I'll walk you back to the hotel.'

'Fair enough.' She lifted up the glass. 'A final toast. To many more hours together — dancing.'

'Just dancing?'

'To many more hours together,' Maggi amended, 'with some of them spent dancing.' They drained their glasses with their arms intertwined, as Maggi insisted that this would make the toast come true. 'Now we should throw the glasses in the fireplace so they can't be used again, but I don't see a fireplace.'

'I'll fix that,' Peter said. He took the two glasses and wrapped them in a napkin. 'Please put these two glasses on my bill,' he told the waiter. He signed the bill after identifying himself to the headwaiter's satisfaction, and they started down the broad staircase past the row of staring portraits.

'What are we going to do with the glasses?' Maggi asked, hanging onto his arm.

'We're going to hunt for a fireplace,' Peter told her. 'I think I remember seeing one in the small lounge in the hotel.'

'I know the room you mean: it looks

like a ski lodge. I think it does have a fireplace. If it doesn't, it should.'

'Right,' Peter agreed. Arm in arm, with the early intimacy of shared secrets and desires, they left the casino. It was dark and they were alone.

Not quite alone. From the dark at the side of the path a cigarette glowed briefly, and footsteps approached them. The cigarette glowed again, and Peter could see the thin face of the man puffing on it.

'Hexcuse me,' the man said. 'Are you not Mistair Carthage?'

'That's right,' Peter said.

'That is good,' the man said, nodding his head slightly. His arm came around in a wide swing at Peter's head. Peter took an instinctive step backward and ducked, pushing Maggi aside at the same time. He felt the wind as the large black object in the man's hand swept past a half-inch from his head. *Missed*, he thought. *Now* . . . He started up and forward on the balls of his feet, to get the attacker before he could recover.

Something soft hit him on the back of the head, and he felt frozen in space.

There must be someone else behind me, he thought. He heard Maggi scream. The softness struck him again and he crumpled, falling into the depths of red-tinted space.

Maggi abruptly stopped screaming.

9

Five men walked around the city of Graustark, followed by five other men. This had been going on for some time, and the followers were getting to be accustomed to the habits of the followed. It had become an easy, monotonous job. This is always a mistake.

The first man went into a hotel barbershop for his usual morning shave. His follower waited outside reading his usual daily paper. It was only after forty minutes had passed that the follower remembered that the barbershop had an exit into the hotel.

The second man, in a hurry that morning, scurried down the street with a paper bag under his arm. The follower was sixty feet behind when the man suddenly turned the corner. Twelve seconds later, passing a stranger in a gray overcoat and fedora, wearing sunglasses, who rounded the corner toward him, the follower himself went around the corner. There was nobody in sight. It took a few minutes for the follower to realize that the paper bag might have held a gray overcoat, fedora, and sunglasses.

The third man went for a swim at one of Alba's famous resort beaches. He never came back.

The fourth man entered a taxi which immediately started out of town. It was almost at the border when the fourth follower discovered that the man had gotten out of the taxi some time before.

The fifth man was more direct. He turned to his follower on the street. 'I believe you're following me,' he said. The follower denied it. 'Yes, I think you're following me,' the man repeated. One ham-like hand suddenly reached out and picked up the tail by his collar. The other hand thrust forward and smote the tail upon his chin. When the tail came to, his man was long gone.

★ ★ ★

They met, these five men, in the back room of a bar. Over large glasses of strong, dark beer, often refilled, they slapped each other on the back and congratulated themselves on their cleverness. They talked over old times and told tall stories of their separate adventures.

'Remember that time in Frankfurt — Piggy couldn't open the safe, so we pulled the truck up and took it with us?'

'It was a jewelry store in Florence. We set off a tear-gas alarm, and then the fuzz walked right into it while we scrammed out the back.'

'He got it at a heist in Hoboken. Two slugs in the leg, and he still managed to drive twelve hundred miles down to Miami before he stopped.'

'So he decided he had a grievance against the syndicate, and he hit one of the big boys for forty thousand and made them eat it.'

The stories went on for some time.

After a time, when the beer passed slowly and the reminiscences had pauses, the one who had called the meeting held up his hand. 'Okay, you guys, let's knock it off for a while and I'll tell you why you're here.'

'Yeah,' one of them said, applauding with his beer glass on the table. 'Let's hear it. Tell the tale.'

'I have gathered you boys and your respective gangs here together to enable us to pull off a caper that will make much profit for all of us.'

A short, hairy member of the group, who was clad only in a bathing suit, noisily drained his glass and refilled it from a pitcher on the table. 'We figured that,' he said. 'What about some facts?'

'Cool it, Benjy. Facts are what I'm here to give you I'll make it short and sweet. We're going to knock over Alba.'

Benjy, who was draining his glass again, spluttered some of the beer onto the table. 'What?' he demanded. 'We're going to what?'

'Knock over Alba.'

'You mean the casino,' someone else demanded.

'No, Alba. The whole place.' Benjy the Mug put both of his hands palm down on the table softly, with no slapping sound. 'I think short-and-sweet isn't going to be good enough. I think, Fudge, that you'd better explain in more detail.'

Mickey Fuggio and his brother Johnny were the two halves of a team known as the Fudge brothers. As the negotiating half, Mickey was at the meeting, Johnny was home with the troops.

'What I mean,' Mickey explained, 'it is simple.'

Big Joe lifted his six-foot-six frame out of the chair and picked up his beer mug, which looked like a shot glass in his hands. 'A toast,' he proposed, 'to the knockover of Alba. Ho ho.' He sat down.

Fuggio took a deep, patient breath. 'What I mean, I got a proposition to put before you what would make it simple for us to knock over Alba.'

'Let's start,' Benjy suggested reasonably, 'with an explanation of what you mean by knocking over Alba. You can't knock over a country — not even one this small.'

'Okay. That's true. But you can knock over everything worth knocking over: the casino, the bank, the jewelry stores, the two hotels where the society types stay. That's what I mean by knocking over Alba. When we're finished, there won't be anything else worth hitting in the whole damn country. What I mean.'

'By damn,' Big Joe said. 'That would be a knockover of Alba. Bigger than birds, that would.'

'How?' asked Benjy. 'What about the fuzz?'

'The police force of Alba will be taken care of for us. We got friends on this job.'

'Yeah? How big a cut do the friends get?'

Mickey the Fudge showed all of his teeth in what he thought was a smile. 'The friends get a finder's fee and their fair share for keeping the fuzz off us while we do the job. A flat twenty-five percent.'

Benjy nodded. 'Oh,' he said, looking like the character in the cartoon who suddenly has the light bulb appear over his head. 'Is that what you mean?'

'What I mean,' Fudge agreed.

'One quarter of the job siphoned off as a finder's fee before we even start. This don't no more sound too good.'

'Not just a finder's fee. Also for keeping the gendarmes off our back. Also they're fencing the stuff for us.'

'Ho!' Big Joe chortled. 'It sounds good. What's the take?'

That was the sort of question Fuggio could understand. He pulled a brown paper envelope out of his pocket and read off a list of figures from the back. 'From the casino, five million; from the bank, two million; from the jewelry stores, three to five million in first-quill stones; from the two hotels — safes and rooms of the swank guests — something around a million each. That's a total of between twelve and fifteen million. What I mean is like it would leave between nine and ten million for us after the quarter is taken.'

'Giving a quarter will be an unusual experience for me, but I'm willing to try anything once,' Benjy said. He looked around for approval, but nobody seemed to care. Big Joe did some quick addition on his fingers; then a thought occurred to him. 'Say,' he demanded, 'million what?'

'What's that?' Fuggio asked.

'The job's good for ten million what? Dollars? Pounds? Drachmae? Guilders? Marks? Yen?'

'Dollars,' Fuggio assured him.

'How do we split?' Benjy asked.

'Even-up, depending on the size of the gang each of us brings into it. We can figure that later. What I want is to know, you all in?'

'Hell, yes.'

'Sure.'

'Count me in.'

'I'm with you!'

'Good,' Fuggio said. 'Now, here's the plan . . . '

10

Pad. Pad. Pad. Pad. Pad.

Peter was in a fishnet sack, held at head and foot and swinging softly from side to side.

Pad. Pad. Pad. Pad. Pad.

The steady motion was lulling, and full consciousness seemed to elude him. His mind kept rising to thought and then drifting off to bright-colored illusion. His dreams were confused and unpleasant.

Pad. Pad. Pad. Pad. Pad.

Now he was going up. His body was tilted head-down, and his feet preceded him into the air. The swaying motion increased, and the weight of his body dug the netting hard into his left ear. This woke him. His neck was twisted, with his chin shoved savagely against the side of his collarbone. Each swing of the fishnet sack crammed his chin deeper into his shoulder. The pain in his neck and shoulder competed for immediate attention with the raw agony of the hemp digging into his ear. Without really being aware of where he was, Peter tried to shift his position to end the pain, but the flexible net and the rhythmic motion seemed to allow only one posture.

Pad. Thunk. Pad. Thunk. Pad. Thunk. Thunk. Pad. Thunk.

He was being carried up some sort of staircase. The way was narrow, and the steady swinging was now knocking him against one of the walls. The staircase seemed to be circular, and the wall was stone. At one particularly narrow point in each cycle, the netting — and Peter — thunked against the wall twice before going back to the pattern.

Gritting his teeth to avoid making a sound, Peter opened his eyes. At first, he thought that he must either be blind-folded or have gone blind, but then his eyes started picking up the dim light. Around the next bend, where a small window was set into the stone wall of the staircase, Peter got his first good view of the proceedings. He, in his net sack, was being carried by two men in brown robes. Behind him, two more men in brown robes were carrying another net sack. The robes were the sort that monks wear.

Peter tried twisting around again, and found why he hadn't been able to. His hands were tied behind him, and his legs were tied together. The monk holding the head part of the sack glared down at him as he twisted. Peter tried to glare back, but was too weak and disoriented to manage more than a brief leer. The glaring monk had a thin, scarred face, set off by a large, greasy beard. His left ear was notched.

Since the glarer knew that Peter was awake, he had nothing to lose by trying to get some information from him. Peter tried to decide what the most logical question would be when you wake to find yourself tied up in a fishnet being lugged up a flight of stairs by an evil-looking monk.

'Hey,' he called, 'what's happening?'

The rear monk lowered his head to within a few inches of Peter's. '*Ese eh cder gib asit terrag,*' he barked, spewing the odor of garlic and dead fish in Peter's face.

'May I assume that you don't speak English?' Peter asked.

'*Sreta wanton*,' the monk snarled, jerking the fishnet. The monk in front turned around and glared at his buddy and at Peter. With this, the procession continued upstairs.

At the top of the stairs, the monks turned left and padded down a corridor. Peter counted twenty-seven pads before they stopped and, opening a wooden door, tossed the sack containing Peter into a small cell. They tossed the second sack in on top of him and then slammed the door and padded off down the corridor. As the sounds went off into the distance, Peter heard the group start a Latin chant.

'Oof,' the sack on top of Peter said.

Peter rolled over. 'Hello there. I seem to have gotten you into a mess, haven't I?'

The other sack bent in the middle as Maggi tried to sit up. 'What happened?'

'We've been kidnapped. We've been wrapped, tied, sealed, and delivered. The big question of the moment is: who is giving us to whom, and why.'

Maggi groaned. 'My head! Oh God, my

143

head hurts. It feels like — no, I don't even want to think of what it feels like.' She lay back down and straightened out. 'There. It feels better if I don't try to move. Can you tell me what's happening?' She tried to keep her voice level, but Peter could detect the beginning of a sob in it.

'I can't tell you any more than I just did,' Peter said, keeping his voice as even and encouraging as he could. 'Somebody wants to talk to me, or us. He obviously doesn't want to hurt us,' he lied, 'or he'd have done so already.' He carefully avoided the thought that the somebody in question might not want to hurt them until after they had talked.

'That sounds logical,' Maggi said, fighting back the edge of hysteria. 'But what do you think they want with me?'

'I think that what they probably want is with me, and you got picked up as an extra because you were there. So it's all my fault. I'm sorry.' The fishnet was starting to dig into his shoulder, so he rolled over. 'If I'd had any idea that this was going to happen . . . ' He let the sentence trail off lamely.

Maggi's thin body was stretched taut through the two layers of fishnet that separated her from Peter. Her back was arched, and the fine muscles in her arms and legs were braced tight in a physical defense against the mental condition of hysteria. 'Don't blame yourself,' she said. Then, after a slight pause, she added, in the tightly-controlled voice of a five-year-old child who thinks she's been punished unjustly, 'But I do wish I knew what was happening.' A tremor ran through her body, and she started sobbing softly. 'I'm sorry,' she said.

'Don't be,' Peter said. 'I wish I had your control.'

'Don't be s-silly. Y-you're not the one who's crying.'

'I would be,' Peter assured her, feeling slightly hysterical himself, 'only I've had more practice at being in this situation than you have. Being captured and tied up by villains is as natural for me as jumping around on stage with nothing but a leotard on is for you. If the positions were reversed, I'd be the one crying.'

Maggi twisted herself into a more

comfortable position and lay there for a long moment, thinking. 'What are we going to do?' she asked.

Peter had been testing his bonds, and discovered that his hands and feet were tied with thick tape of some sort. 'If I could get my hands untied, I could get us out of these fishnets, but it doesn't look like I can get my hands untied. So I guess we're going to wait here until one of those monks comes back to untie us. Now, don't worry. I have a few tricks up my sleeve — as soon as I can get at my sleeve. Just think of what an exciting experience this will be to tell your grandchildren about.'

'I'll try to keep that in mind. Do you really think we're going to get out of this?'

'I always have,' Peter assured her.

The soft padding sound of sandal-clad feet returned to the corridor; in a few seconds, the door was opened, and five monks came through. Two of them grabbed each of the prisoners and stood them up. The fifth monk pulled a long, S-shaped blade from beneath his robes and, with a scowl so deep that his drooping mustache almost touched points under his chin, sliced up the fishnet sacks and cut through the tape around their wrists. 'Nes nebnod!' he growled and the monks withdrew, taking the fishnet refuse with them.

'They're certainly a nasty bunch,' Maggi said, stripping the remnants of tape from around her wrists and legs. 'What sort of monks do you think they are?'

'I somehow get the impression that they aren't in any of the recognized orders,' Peter said. 'A monastery is an awfully good front: who knows what goes on inside?'

'I should think they'd send inspectors around.'

'What 'they'?' Peter asked. 'There are a lot of monasteries around that aren't associated with any church, so they have no higher-ups to keep tabs on them. It looks like this one either went bad or has been taken over. I think we'll soon find out which.'

'Cheerful,' Maggi said, sitting on a stone shelf that ran the length of the back wall of the cell — about seven feet. 'All right, let's hear it.'

'What?'

'How we're going to get out of here.'

'I haven't quite figured that out yet,' Peter admitted, 'but be of good cheer — I'm working on it.' He walked around the cell, poking at the walls and inspecting the hinges on the door.

'Find anything?' Maggi asked.

'Yes. They used a good quality of mortar in these old walls.'

Maggi rubbed her hand across the wall. 'I don't suppose it would help if I got hysterical, would it?'

Peter sat down beside her and put his arm around her shoulders. 'I'm sorry. Flippancy can get to be a bad habit.'

A pair of sandals flopped down the corridor and stopped in front of their cell. A small hatch at the bottom of the door lifted, and a tray was slid through. The hatch slammed shut and the sandals padded away.

Peter went over to get the tray and brought it back to the shelf. 'Well, at least they're planning to feed us.'

Two pewter bowls, two china mugs, and two soup spoons sat on the wooden tray. Two paper napkins were tucked into one of the handles.

'I didn't think I was hungry, but that food smells good,' Maggi said. 'What is it, do you know?'

'It looks like some sort of stew. The stuff in the mugs smells like tea to me.'

'Stew sounds fine,' Maggi said. 'Besides, I doubt if the chef will allow substitutions.' She reached for the bowl.

'Wait a second,' Peter said. 'Those things are hot.' He took one of the napkins and wrapped it around a bowl, then handed it across the tray. 'Here you are, Miss Blaire; I hope you find your dinner satisfactory.'

'Thank you, Mister Carthage, you are most kind.' Maggi took the bowl carefully by the napkin, tucked her legs under her, and started to eat with the appetite and abandon of a twelve-year-old tomboy.

Peter picked up his own bowl and leaned back against the wall, watching Maggi eat. She was, he decided, quite a woman. Her dress looked like — well, it looked like she'd worn it overnight while being tossed around in a fishnet sack. Her face was dirty, her hair was matted, her stockings had gaping holes where scratched knee or braised calf came through, she had been kidnapped and locked up in a cell by a bunch of maniac monks, her life was in danger, and she sat there calmly eating. Despite all that, she still managed to look beautiful. If it was humanly possible, Peter told himself, he was going to get her out of this,

'You're not eating,' Maggi said, looking up at him.

'Sorry, I was thinking.'

'About how to get us out of here? I'm sorry I interrupted. But you really should eat. It'll keep up your strength. Besides, this is pretty good chow mein.'

'Chow mein?' He took a spoonful. 'Well, I'll be damned. Fascinating. Chow mein and tea.'

'Why do you find that fascinating?'

'It reminds me of something I was told recently by a Mister Smith.'

'Does that help? Well, I have confidence in you. If it's possible to get out of here, you'll find the way. Tell me if I can do anything.' Maggi smiled at him and sipped her tea.

The cell door swung open and a seven-foot man in leather armor filled the doorway. 'You come 'long with me. Not you, Missy, you wait here.'

11

The two gangs, spies and thieves, continued along their different paths to destiny.

Item:
The guards for the Royal Alban Paperworks assembled in a small lecture room. From behind the lectern a thin, dapper man smiled down at them. 'Good morning, gentlemen,' he said. 'My name is Mister Valiant. I am a representative of the Marvel and Duck Corporate Protective Association. If you'll give me a few minutes of your time, I'd like to demonstrate a device that we believe will revolutionize the field of plant protection and security.' He carefully set his attaché case down, opened it, and pulled out an object that looked like a thick, silver fountain pen with a knob on the top and a clip on the side.

'This,' Mister Valiant said, waving the silver sausage in the air, 'is the Guard Assurance and Protective Device. When hooked in with the Guard Control Master Display Unit in the plant security office, it enables a guard in trouble, or needing immediate advice or support, to get it by merely pushing this button — ' He indicated the knob on top. ' — and talking. Pushing the button will cause the unit's exact location to flash on a screen in the Guard Control Master Display Unit, and will turn on a sensitive microphone in the Guard Assurance and Protective Device.

'We are placing these devices here for a ninety-day evaluation trial. The master unit will be installed tomorrow, at which time you will each receive one of these — ' He waved the sausage. ' — to carry with you at all times. Are there any questions?'

Item:
The little man with the stiff mustache and the wispy beard was the color of ingrained dirt. His faded, washed-out coveralls were splotchy with tar, his shoes were crusted with sand, and his brimmed and flattened leather hat smelt strongly of decades of sweat. He possessed great dignity.

'I dinna if I can do it,' he said sadly. 'It's not the money, you understand. I just don't see how I can let Betsy out of my sight for that long.'

Mickey sighed patiently. 'It's only two days, Mister Schact, and I promise to take good care of it — her.'

'You sure I couldn't come along and do the job for you? Then there'd be no problem.'

'I'd like that, Mister Schact, really I would, but it's impossible. I've explained that. This is a classified government project, and there just isn't enough time to get you a clearance.'

'Well,' Schact said, patting Betsy's side, 'my girl here is finicky. I'd have to teach you how to handle her.'

'I was counting on that,' Mickey told him. 'You show me how to run her and take care of her, and I'll treat her like she was my own. You have my solemn word.'

'Well, seeing as how it's for the government and all . . . All right, you can use her.' Schact paused to scrape a flake of rust off his fifty-ton charcoal-burning steamroller. 'But mind now, treat her gentle.'

Item:

Frickel's Quality Jewelry Store — Fine Stones Bought & Sold (New York, Paris, London, Graustark, Monaco) was just closing for the night when the tiny old man with the large nose and the wide-brim felt hat came through the door. Mister Raulf, a junior clerk who was a serious contender for the Year's Most Unctuous Salesperson Award, slithered over and looked down his narrow nose.

'Yes?' he nasaled. 'What may we do for you?'

The tiny old man glared at Raulf's middle. 'Get out of my way!' he suggested.

'Why — ' Raulf took a step backward before this onslaught. ' — what do you mean?'

The old man took a small loose-leaf notebook out of his jacket pocket. 'Uncooperative clerk,' he said, jotting an obscure sign on a page of the book.

'Now, well, wait a minute. Uncooperative for what? I mean, what do you want to do? All I want,' Raulf said, doing his best to look soulless, 'is to be of assistance. Who are you?'

'Fire inspector,' the little man told him.

Raulf was doubtful. 'I know the fire inspector,' he said.

'For the insurance syndicate. We're doing a survey of conditions in all the buildings on this block.' He pulled out a badge, a pass, and several important-looking documents, and waved the batch in Raulf's face. 'I have to check a few things.'

'I'll have to get the manager to give you permission,' Raulf said.

'Fine, fine. Bring him out.'

'Mister Van Guerlik is home. I will have to call him, and he will have to come down here.'

'Now, come on. I don't have that kind of time. There are forty other stores on this block, and I have till the end of the week to finish the survey. Look — I just want to walk around: you come with me.'

'I don't think that would be proper.'

'Well,' the little man sneered, 'if you don't have the authority . . . '

'It's not a question of that at all. Of course I can — do. What do you want to see?'

'The rooms, ceilings, and walls — that's all.'

'Fine. Come with me.'

They walked from room to room. The main room first, then the private viewing room for special clients, then the two back rooms. The little man took constant notes and asked an occasional question. 'That line,' he asked once, indicating electric tape on the wall, 'is it part of the fire alarm?'

'I wouldn't know,' Raulf answered stiffly, making it clear that such knowledge was below him.

'That's all right,' the little man told him, pulling out a small, curved pipe and tamping tobacco into it. 'Nothing to be ashamed of. A lot of people wouldn't know. Of course,' he reflected, 'most of them don't work here. Got a chart or diagram of some kind?'

'Oh yes,' Raulf said. 'I remember seeing one. I'll get it.' He went over to a desk and started riffling through the drawers. 'Ah, here it is.'

'Thank you.' The little man took the diagram and spread it out on the desk. 'I

157

see. That line is a burglar alarm, this one is the fire alarm. Ah! And there's the safe. Tell me,' he said, walking over to the wall which, according to the diagram, concealed the safe, 'how does it — ah!' He jiggled a thingummy on the wall, and it quietly slid open.

'Say! You can't do . . . '

'That line there — fire detector for inside the safe?'

'Why no, that's the alarm line to the police station.'

'Ah, I see.' The little man wrote several lines in his notebook. 'An Ouiga Vault, I see.'

'That's right. Say — how can a fire start in an airless safe?'

The little man rubbed the side of his nose. 'The ways of nature are mysterious,' he told Raulf, 'and not to be questioned by mortal man. There are some things — ' He put his hat on. ' — man was not meant — ' He stuck the notebook back in his pocket. ' — to know!' He exited through the front door, leaving this powerful but familiar phrase ringing in Raulf's ears.

Item:

L'Hotel Grand Claud, one of the triumvirate of luxury hotels fronting the square by the casino, was preparing to wake up and face the new day. The night manager was filling out the last of the many forms that a night manager has to spend most of his time filling out, and starting to anticipate his nice long day in bed.

Ting.

'Hello! Anybody here? Front! Desk! Hello!'

Ting.

Feeling a strong sense of regret that he had let the clerk leave early, the night manager stumbled out of his office and faced the irate guest who was starting to play 'Johnny One-Note' on the bell. 'Yes, sir,' the manager said, in that voice of desire-to-serve that is indicative of a first-class hotel anywhere in the world. 'How may I assist you?'

Room 1704 (Mister Benjamin to his face) stopped his bell solo and produced a weary smile from somewhere deep in his character. 'Good morning. Before I retire to the wonderful room you have supplied me, I would like to put something in the hotel safe. I'm sorry I woke you. If it isn't too great an inconvenience, would you open the safe for me?'

Why, the manager grumped as he came around the desk, *do they always resort to sarcasm at this hour of the morning?* 'This way, please,' he said, leading the way to the room at the side of the lobby. 'Please stand behind the counter while I open the safe.'

Mister 1704 Benjamin, nicknamed 'The Mug,' leaned heavily on his side of the counter. 'You have my solemn word.'

The manager turned around and, methodically shielding the dial from view with his body, started to open the safe door that took up one wall of the room. He worked quickly and with the precision of long practice.

Also working quickly and precisely, and with absolute silence, Benjy the Mug put together the sections of a collapsible aluminum rod that he took from under his jacket. Holding the extended rod much like a fly-casting pole over the manager's head, Benjy stared intently into the little mirror set into the tip. Every time the manager stopped spinning the dial and swung it gently around to a number, Benjy mouthed the number silently as he committed it to memory.

'There!' the manager said, and started swinging the locking handle down to release the catches. Benjy silently agreed and pulled the extension rod back and started to section it.

All the sections but two were apart and under his coat, and the last two were being attended to, when the manager suddenly turned around. 'Well, Mister Benjamin, if you'll give me whatever you have to put in the safe, we'll . . . What on earth is that thing in your hand?'

Benjy glared at him sourly. 'It's an extension rod. I was using it to read the numbers over your shoulder while you opened the safe.'

'Well!' the manager huffed. 'No need to get nasty about it. What did you want to put in the safe?'

'Never mind,' Benjy said. 'I think I'll

take my business elsewhere.' He turned around and walked out of the manager's life — for a while.

09101 Precedence. The digest is accept
09102 able. Branch Group A is concluding
09103 its preparations adequately. Branch
09104 Group B is concluding its prepara
09105 tions adequately. Both groups, there
09106 fore, are concluding its / their prep
09107 arations adequately. I scan. I scan.
09108 I scan. Qwertyuiop.

12

The big man closed the cell door and preceded Peter down the stone corridor. He walked with the curious gliding motion of an ice skater, or of one walking on glass. They walked around, down, up and across, threading through the stone corridors and staircases like Theseus in search of the Minotaur. Finally they came to rest in a small stone anteroom. At the door stood two guards, in brown monks' robes, with submachine guns resting in the crooks of their arms.

'You stay here, not move. I go,' the leather giant stated.

'What's . . . ' But the big man was already out the door. Peter sat down on the long, wooden bench and stared glumly at the guards. They stared back.

'Hello,' Peter said.

They continued staring.

'You don't speak English, I take it?'

Stare.

Peter looked around for something to do besides lock eyes with a pair of mute guards. He gave a half-hearted thought toward how easy it would be to get by the two guards in an escape attempt, or get shot trying and end this thing one way or the other, but he couldn't take the chance while there was any hope — however small — of getting Maggi out of this in one piece. Besides, he was kind of curious as to exactly what was going on, who had grabbed him, and why. Not that finding out would do him any good.

On the bench in the other corner was a small pile of paper. Peter slid across and found that it was a bunch of magazines. He found himself looking at the pile for some time before he could bring himself to pick one up. *Oh, fine*, he thought, *I'm trapped in the waiting room of a medieval medicine man*. The magazine he picked up was in some middle-European language that looked like it could almost be understood if you'd only try a little harder. The pages were full of color photographs — mostly reds and browns — of healthy, apple-cheeked maidens, singly and in large, ordered groups, going through complicated calisthenics and looking happy. They seemed to be making a point of looking happy. It was almost as if someone was standing behind the camera and ordering them to look happy. It was very depressing.

The next magazine was in Chinese and on rice paper. There were, Peter found after a quick examination, no pictures.

The third was on glossy paper and in English. It was a copy of the *Computer Technology Weekly* for the week of March 19, 1964. Peter picked this one up and started to read. He quickly found that, from the layman's point of view, it wasn't any more in English than the rice paper magazine he'd looked at before.

The far door opened and Peter's seven-foot guide beckoned. 'You, come.'

'No, no,' Peter said, getting up. 'You're supposed to say, 'The doctor will see you now.''

'Doctor, he want see you now,' the giant agreed amiably. Slightly shocked, Peter followed him through the door. They went down yet another corridor and around the corner. The giant stood aside and waved Peter into the room. Peter's impression was of a white area with white cabinets, white machines, and white-frocked men.

One of the men came over to Peter. 'Good afternoon. Will you please come over here; the doctor is just about ready for you.'

This, Peter decided, was carrying cooperation a little too far. 'What if I say no?' he asked. 'I don't want to go over there.'

'*Nosredna!*' the white-frocked one barked. Two large, leather-clad arms wrapped around Peter from behind, and his giant escort lifted him effortlessly a foot in the air. 'Just over this way,' the white-coated one said to Peter, his bland expression unchanged. He walked across the room and Peter — a foot in the air — followed.

'If you'd be kind enough to just sit over here,' White-coat asked politely. Leather-giant dropped Peter into the indicated chair and took up a guard position behind him.

Peter smiled. 'Glad to oblige.'

A white door opened at the far side of

the room and a tall man entered. He was clad in brown monk's garb with the curious addition of a thin gold lacing around all the edges. The other people in the room continued what they were doing, but now in a self-conscious way. The murmur of conversation stopped, and everyone sort of stepped aside as the gold-edged monk strode through the room. It was an atmosphere that Peter recognized, that of a group of second lieutenants performing their normal duties with a general in the room.

Aha, Peter thought. *It must be the mother superior.*

The tall monk went behind a screen in the corner of the room. When he emerged a few seconds later, he had exchanged his brown habit for a white smock — also embroidered with gold thread. Rubbing his hands together in a gesture of eager anticipation, he approached Peter. 'Ah, Mister Carthage; yes, yes. I've been looking forward to meeting you for some time. I must say, this is an honor.'

'Must you?' Pete asked, smiling up at him.

'Indeed. You are possessed of some

information I need. That is why you have been brought here. Allow me to introduce myself; I am Doctor Chang Hu.'

'It's a pleasure — or, at any rate, an experience — to meet you, Marquis. Being a guest in your house provides no end of surprises.'

'You know me!' Chang Hu exclaimed. 'But I expected no less. The question that must be answered is: How much else do you know?'

Peter started to get up, but was pushed back down by the giant standing behind him. 'I don't suppose you'd believe me if I offered to tell you, so we could leave out the obligatory torture? I've never been very fond of torture.'

'Ah, Mister Carthage,' Chang Hu said, raising one long finger in illustration, 'I agree completely with you on that point.' Peter noticed that the nail on the raised finger was painted gold, as were the other nails in the clenched hand. 'Torture is an invidious method of getting information. It suffers from many disadvantages, both to the torturer and the, um, torturee. Then there is always the point that it is really impossible to tell how reliable the information that is obtained by physical duress is without actually testing it — which can be an expensive proposition.' He allowed his finger to drop back down to his side. 'No, Mister Carthage, all in all I don't think we shall resort to torture to extract the required data. I hope you find that reassuring.'

Peter found it more puzzling than anything else, as he didn't assume that the doctor-Marquis would settle for merely asking him questions with a stenographer's notebook on his lap. He was, however, willing to wait for an answer. He said, 'I'm relieved that your attitude is more modern than the primitive, medieval appearance of this place would indicate.'

Chang Hu nodded. 'It doesn't look as though the Inquisition would have been too out of place here; as, I believe, in fact it wasn't. There are a few rooms in the cellar that indicate a possible harsher use in past ages than wine storage. Well, we must march on with the times.'

'What has Miss Blaire to do with all this?' Peter asked.

'The charming young lady who is, at present, your roommate? She was taken for the same reason Everest was climbed — she was there. Don't worry, she will not be harmed.'

'Are you going to let her go?'

'She will be released at the same moment that you yourself are. You have my word.'

'Thanks,' Peter said. He had a fairly clear idea of when the Marquis would be willing to release him, but there was no use in arguing about it. Something more drastic would be needed.

'Now that we've had this delightful little chat,' Chang Hu said, 'if you'd be good enough to climb up on this little table, we'll proceed with the job of eliciting the necessary information from you.'

'What . . . '

The two leather-covered arms grabbed him and lifted him in the air. His feet were grabbed by one of the white-coats, and he was flipped, like a sack of potatoes, onto a wheeled patient table next to the chair. Four men, each at a limb, mauled him into position and flipped the leather restraining straps around his chest and legs. In a second, the straps were tight, and he was securely fastened onto the table.

The Marquis Chang Hu came over and stood staring down at him. His lean, drawn, thin face, which came down like a triangle from the top of his bald head to the tip of his thin, pointed beard, was wearing a properly inscrutable expression, but there was the faintest hint of an incredibly evil smile hovering around his bloodless lips. 'Thank you for being so cooperative, Mister Carthage,' he said.

Peter twisted around to test the limits of the leather, but whoever had designed the little table had known what he was doing — there was no way to get enough slack to put up any form of resistance. 'Always glad to oblige,' he said calmly.

'You have the proper philosophic attitude,' the Marquis commended, his half-closed gray eyes glinting down at Peter. 'It is time, as the old adage goes, to relax and enjoy it.' The Marquis' slender, bony hands were at work on something out of Peter's line of sight. Then they came into view, holding the object they had been occupied with — a thin, glass hypodermic syringe with a two-inch needle.

The Marquis held the syringe up to the light and inspected it closely. This gave Peter a chance to also inspect it closely. He didn't find its look particularly esthetic or appealing. It glinted in the light: the glass tube glinted and the silver-bright needle glinted. The fluid in the tube, marked off by black cc-division lines, was a bright green. There were many cc marks on the tube before it reached the point where it ran out of green.

'Thank you for the thought,' Peter said, finding himself unable to keep his eyes off the gleaming syringe, 'but I've already had all my shots for the year. Not that I don't appreciate what you're doing for me.'

'Yes, yes,' Marquis Chang Hu agreed. 'Don't worry — this won't hurt you a bit.' He squeezed the plunger slightly, forcing a bead of green liquid to appear at the tip of the needle. 'Swab off the inner arm please; I need a vein.'

Two white-coated men released Peter's right arm, rolled up the shirtsleeve, and rubbed the inner arm above the elbow with a cotton swab dipped in alcohol. Then they strapped the wrist back down to the table so that the swabbed area was exposed.

Peter's mouth felt completely dry, and from somewhere deep inside of him, he could feel his heart beating triple-time. The muscles in his stomach and groin were busy tying themselves into the best knots they could manage with his body tied down. *I do believe*, Peter told himself, *that I'm undergoing the classical fear reaction. Surprise surprise.* The thing that he found interesting was that his mind remained completely analytical even after his body started reacting with panic. It would help, he decided, if he knew what that green stuff was.

'The substance you are staring at,' Chang Hu said, as if reading his mind, 'is a mixture of sodium pentothal and an ancient Tibetan drug known as *Yat-ga tanga sippu*. This is the first step in the process.'

'The first step,' Peter repeated.

'Yes. This will enable us to get enough preliminary information to correctly program step two, which will drain your brain of all the information it contains. That is, all that interests us.'

'Swell,' Peter said.

'It is quick and efficient,' Chang Hu said, bringing the needle down to the level of the table, 'and, oh yes, painless. A point that should please you.' He pulled the skin on Peter's forearm taut and, in one swift motion, jabbed the needle in. For a second he twisted it to find a vein; then he slowly pushed the plunger in, forcing the green fluid into Peter's bloodstream.

'I don't . . . ' Peter said. Then his ears started to ring, and the sound swept up like a mighty waterfall and carried him over the edge. He sank deeper and deeper inside himself, surrounded by sound and a persistence of vision. Somewhere in front of him, figures, as if cast on a frosted-glass screen, moved slowly and did things of no importance. The tall Chang Hu slowly stood up and moved away from him. Then he was left alone for a time, perhaps a long time. Then a cloud of white-coated men surrounded him and prodded him and squeezed at him and went away again.

The noise lowered and lowered and lowered and smothered itself until it was gone. And all was dully quiet. And all was a uniform shade of gray. And there was no time.

— What is your name? a voice demanded.

Funny about that voice. Peter wondered briefly where it was coming from. And who it was talking to. Oh, well, it didn't matter to him — just a minor intrusion on his formless existence. He would ignore it.

— Peter Carthage.

There was no answer. Who was answering? That didn't matter either. Peter would just be there and listen while these voices went on somewhere over him. Under him?

— Where do you work?

— War, Incorporated.

— What do you do for them? What is your job?

— I am an expediter. I head teams.

— Head teams?

(You can't get an answer like that; you have to phrase it as a question).

(Even if you phrase it as a question, he probably can't get much more specific than that in this stage. Go on.)

— Who do you work for? Who is your superior?

— The head of War, Incorporated is Doctor Steadman.

Something deep in Peter's subconscious felt a stirring at the questions he was overhearing. They somehow seemed familiar — overly familiar.

— Describe this Doctor Steadman in terms that you recognize and identify him by.

The voices continued to drone on, and the consciousness that was Peter lost interest and drifted away. Soon he was unable to hear or perceive anything at all. On a different level of consciousness, his body — Satanists might say, his soulless body — continued to answer questions, if they were direct and simple enough.

Time passed.

'I don't think I'm going to like this,' Peter said. Then he realized that everything was in a different position than it was what seemed to him only a second before. He remembered drifting, and the sound of voices.

There was a gross chuckle, a sound that combined the harshness of an old man with the wondrous joy of a child, and included a touch of pure evil. Peter looked around and found the Marquis Chang Hu standing by the table. 'It is over. As I said, quick, efficient, and painless. We now have enough background information to begin the second half of the operation.'

'The second half. Then this is just an intermission. Time to go out and have a smoke before the curtain goes up.'

'We'll do better than that for you, Mister Carthage. We'll give you an evening break and take up again tomorrow morning. Sleep well.' Chang Hu turned abruptly and walked away. A group of white-coats leaped at Peter's bonds and untied him, then leaped back like well-operated puppets.

'Well,' Peter said, and swung his legs over the side of the table. He pushed his arms under him and sat up. All at once a trip-hammer inside his head went off and started pounding its way through his skull, trying to break a hole through right above his left ear. 'Wow,' Peter said, shaking his head. 'Some painless.' He pressed his hand against his temple and found that the pressure helped some, but not much. 'Anybody got an aspirin?'

'*Ko octap*,' one of the white-coats explained, and gently pushed him back down onto the table. A few seconds later, another one brought him a glass of water and a large, red pill. Figuring that nothing could be much worse than the pain in his head, Peter gladly swallowed the pill. A few seconds later, like a wave coming in from the Sea of Pain, a stomach cramp hit him, doubling him up on the table. It passed, and a second came, and a third, and a fourth; but each was less severe than the last, and, like an ebb tide, they soon lessened to the point of harmlessness and passed. With them, Peter discovered, his headache had also passed.

Peter sat up again and slid off the table. 'What's in that pill?' he asked. 'It's kind of a drastic cure, but it works, and it works fast.'

'*Refinajem*,' the white-coat stated, '*nerval*.'

'Nerval indeed,' Peter agreed.

The leather giant, whom Peter was almost beginning to accept as an old friend among this crowd of kidnappers, escorted him back to his cell and secured the door behind him.

* * *

Maggi was asleep on a threadbare piece of army blanket laid over the stone ledge. When he came in she rolled over and sat up, stretching her arms. 'Hrumph. Peter. Peter! What happened? Where'd they take you? How are you? I'm glad you're back!'

'I'm glad I'm back, too,' Peter admitted. He sat down on the ledge, and Maggi snuggled next to him and put her arms around his chest.

'Well, what happened?' she asked.

Peter spent the next half-hour telling her what he could remember of his experiences in the white room, and of the doctor-Marquis Chang Hu who seemed to be in charge of the operation. He was very careful to point out that it was entirely his fault that she was there. She was just as quick to disagree.

'That's positively silly,' she said. 'You had something they wanted, and I happened to be there when they decided to take it. It's unfortunate, but not in any way that I can see your fault. It could just as easily have been something I had that they wanted — a diamond pendant, for example, or the secret plans to my next dance. Besides, you're going to get us out of here. You promised.'

'In the face of such sublime confidence, no man could fail,' Peter said, hoping it was true. Maggi went back to sleep curled up in Peter's arms, but Peter stayed up most of the night, staring across the dark cell at rough-hewn stone walls and thinking sad thoughts about the approaching morning.

12345 Test of mechanized escape vehicles.
12346 Programming not complete for sub-
12347 marine guidance. Checkout needed
12348 on balloon. Have prepared for Car
12349 thage. Good meat — bad wine.

13

Ted Ursa sat in a canvas director's chair, his brown legs sticking out below the khaki Bermuda shorts, while on the field in front of him a squad of Alban policemen in fatigue uniforms thrust at each other with bayonet-tipped shotguns. Ted barked out the ancient tribal rhythm of the ritualistic dance: 'Hah — hoh — heh — thrust — guard — return . . . Up there — keep it up, there. Watch your guard. Hah — hoh — heh.'

Professor Perlemutter, bulging out on all sides of his little Lambretta motor scooter, puttered over to Ted and silenced his machine. For a few moments, he stood watching this performance, then he cast himself off the Lambretta and sank down next to Ted.

'Urmph,' he said.

Ted signaled his men to take a break, and they all sat down in little clumps around the field. He asked the Professor,

'That sound you made just now — what does it mean?'

'It was meant to convey the feeling of elation that I always get watching other people work. How are they doing?'

Ted gestured in the air, waving an imaginary sword. 'Bring on your riots!'

'Well, that's very nice,' Professor Perlemutter admitted, 'but are you sure it's riots that we must be wary of?'

'You tell me. Tell them — ' He waved a hand toward the resting men. ' — what to train for. Anyway, if it is riots, we'll be ready for them. I don't think it's going to be riots, mind you; but if it is, we'll be ready for them.'

'I think I get the idea,' Professor Perlemutter said, patting the fringe of hair on his head. 'But we'll try to be ready for them whatever they have in mind.'

'Any word about Peter or Miss Blaire?' Ted asked.

'Nothing. Nothing at all. They seem to have just disappeared. We'll have to assume that they've been taken by — whomever our adversary is.' He shook his head. 'I feel like I'm groping in the dark to find a pack of matches to light a candle so I can find out whether I've gone blind or not.'

'I guess we can only hope that they're still alive,' Ted said.

'The reports of Peter Carthage's death have always been greatly exaggerated in the past,' Professor Perlemutter said firmly, 'and I'm assuming that this will be no exception. At any rate, we can be sure of one thing: Peter now knows a lot more about what and who we're facing than we do.'

'May whatever gods of warriors are left in this modern age get him back here soon to tell us about it,' Ted said, knocking on his hollow-sounding right leg.

'That's an interesting way of knocking on wood,' Perlemutter commented. 'Do you find it increases your luck?'

'Having a hollow leg has some advantages,' Ted admitted. 'This one's aluminum, not wood, but I figure the principle's the same.'

'Where does it join onto the real one?' the Professor asked, his unabashed curiosity always taking precedence over politeness.

'I thought Peter said it was somewhere below the knee, but I don't see it.'

'A marvel of engineering,' Ted told him. 'I'll have you know, I'm wearing an experimental model leg, which is a hell of a thought. The join is right up here.' He traced a line on the smooth brown skin of his thigh, right below the bottom of his Bermuda shorts. 'Just a little above the knee.'

'How does it articulate?' Perlemutter asked. 'I can hardly see where the join is. As a matter of fact, until you pointed it out I didn't see it. I'm still not sure I do.'

'It's well done,' Ted said. 'It should be, it cost enough. Luckily, I didn't have to pay for it myself — the Army did. The join is aided with a bit of cosmetics.' He flexed the knee, moving the leg up and down, and twisted his foot around in a circle. 'You wouldn't believe how long it took me to learn to do that.'

'But if the artificial leg starts above the knee, how do you manage to move both the knee and the foot?' He was staring at the real looking right leg with an expression that must have rivaled the

Pharaoh's when Moses threw down his staff and turned it into a snake.

'Gosh, Doc, I dunno,' Ted said, smiling. 'I just get in and turn the thing on, and off she goes. I don't know how it works. I just got to remember to put gas in it, change the oil every once in a while, and check the tires — that's all.'

'Very funny.' Professor Perlemutter snorted. 'A person tries to indulge his scientific curiosity — without which we'd all be back in the Dark Ages — and everyone makes fun of him, man and boy. Never mind, I didn't want to hear about your leg anyway. You probably couldn't explain it if I did.'

'My dear man,' Ted said, 'you're in a huff. What a splendid thing to watch. What was it you wanted to know?'

'How that leg of yours works, that's what I wanted to know.'

'But of course. I'd be delighted to explain it to you.' Ted lifted the leg. 'The knee and foot joints are operated by a group of small but powerful solenoids, arranged much as the muscles in a real leg are.' He flexed the leg.

'A beautiful job,' Professor Perlemutter said, peering closely at the artificial limb.

'I'm glad you're impressed. I was too, when they showed it to me.'

'What powers it?'

'Small, very powerful, rechargeable batteries. The most expensive part of the leg, not counting the research that produced it. At night, when I go to sleep, I plug the leg in to charge it up for the next day. Wild thought, isn't it?'

'Indeed, I find it fascinating. How do you control the limb?'

'Little sensors built into the solenoids activate them according to how I flex a series of muscles in what's left of my leg — and a few other places.'

'Ah! I see. But — you don't appear to have any wires running to the leg. Don't tell me they're built in.'

Ted laughed. 'No, nothing like that. That's probably the next step, though. These are external. They generate an electronic field, which activates the sensors by tone modulation across a set frequency. Do you follow that?'

'I think so,' Professor Perlemutter said.

'You might say that your leg works by FM radio. A rock and roll radio station broadcasting close enough to you could really set you dancing.'

'That's one of the things that happened on the first few models,' Ted said seriously. 'Spurious radiation from nearby sources caused test legs to twitch or go out of control. But that can't happen anymore. The frequency used now is very high and the signal is coded.'

'It must take a lot of practice to learn to operate one of those things.'

'It does,' Ted verified. 'Months and months.'

'Yes, well, must take a lot of guts, too. Hrrumph.' Perlemutter coughed and looked embarrassed.

'I don't know about that,' Ted said. 'If you've lost a leg and somebody comes along and gives you a chance to walk again — that's worth a lot. Six months learning how to use your leg isn't much compared to forty or fifty years in a wheelchair.'

'You have a point,' Perlemutter conceded, not looking overly convinced. 'When will you be finished drilling these young troopers?'

'Another hour should do it for today,' Ted said.

Perlemutter hauled his bulk out of the chair. 'Good. In two and a half hours we are reporting to Prefect Damarat. I'll meet you downstairs and we'll go up together. Remember — in unity there is strength. Or, as that great revolutionary once put it: We must all hang together, or we will most assuredly all hang, separately.'

'What are we supposed to report on?' Ted asked.

'That's a very good question. Progress is the answer. We're supposed to report on our progress, if any. I have to report on how the newly-formed counterespionage section has been following around a bunch of spies and succeeded in finding absolutely nothing even faintly suspicious — which is in itself suspicious; you have to report that your Special Action Branch is now ready to handle whatever comes up, if whatever comes up happens to be a riot. Which I doubt. Our reports should make Prefect Damarat weep with joy.'

'Well at any rate, they should make him

weep,' Ted agreed. He signaled his men to resume their positions, as Professor Perlemutter puttered off down the road on his overloaded motor scooter.

12666 Bring Carthage. I am ready.

14

Peter woke up the next morning with no memory of having gone to sleep. He was still in the same position: half-sitting up, with Maggi curled up by him, head in his lap. Trying not to wake her, Peter yawned and stretched his arms out to drive some of the sleep from his system. He discovered that the muscles of his back and shoulders had knotted up from their cramped position in his unconsciousness. Now that he was awake, they decided that it was a fine time to start protesting their unreasonable treatment. Peter leaned forward and, putting his arms out to the sides, fists clenched, jerked them rapidly back and forth to get the circulation going again and unknot some of the muscles.

Maggi stirred uneasily and opened her eyes. 'What . . . Is it morning already?'

'Just about,' Peter said. 'I didn't mean to wake you.'

'Don't be silly,' Maggi said, sitting up

and rubbing the sleep out of her eyes. 'I'm surprised I got to sleep at all. It must be the therapeutic effect of being held by you. Say, you weren't sitting up all night wide awake, were you?'

'No, not all night. That is, I was sitting up all night, but I was sound asleep for a good bit of it. The funny thing is, I didn't intend to go to sleep, it just kind of crept up on me.'

'I'm glad you slept,' Maggi said. 'But I wish you had lain down — you must be stiff all over.'

'I am that,' Peter admitted, massaging his arms. 'I wonder when our jailors are going to get here with breakfast.'

'Personally,' Maggi told him, 'I could use a bath. I tell you, if the girls in my high school graduating class could see me now — me, who was voted 'Most Likely To Succeed' — it'd ruin the image for sure.'

'As a matter of fact,' Peter said, 'I was voted 'Most Likely To Enter The Monastery.' Somehow I doubt that this is what they had in mind.'

Maggi did her best to look surprised.

'The monastery? You?'

'It was a private joke, the kind that high school kids love to sneak into yearbooks. 'The Monastery' was the name of a local men's club, known for its bar.'

Maggi sat for a few moments, silent and meditative, looking at the thick wood door which connected the small, stone cell to the outside world. 'What do you think the monks who built this place used a locked cell for? Disciplining anyone who came late for matins?'

Peter ran his hand along the rough wall. 'I don't know,' he told her. 'I would imagine it was a precaution. This place is sort of out of the way. Perhaps the abbot felt it necessary to have some sort of control over the guests they put up for the night.'

Maggi turned around and grabbed his hand. 'Peter! Tell me the truth: do you really think they're going to let us go?'

'I'm sorry, but that's easy to answer. No. Of course not. When they finish questioning me, or whatever it is that they're doing, they'll either put us on ice or get rid of us.'

Maggi shook visibly for a second, and

her nails dug into the side of Peter's hand. 'When I ask you to be honest, I really get it, don't I?'

Peter put his arm around her and pulled her to him in a protective gesture. 'Buck up,' he said, feeling a little foolish. If he could have thought of anything more encouraging to say, he would have. At the moment, things just didn't seem very encouraging.

'What is there to buck up about?' Maggi asked in a dull voice.

'Pessimism is a vice that I usually don't believe in. It's what causes you to give up and die in the snow half a mile from the camp. Well, we're not going to give up. We're going to find a way out of here.'

Ping — ping. Ping, ping, ping — ping, ping, ping, ping. Ping, ping, ping, ping, ping — ping, ping, ping, ping, ping . . .

The sound seemed far away, and somehow sad and alone. Regular pings, evenly spaced in some kind of pattern, they kept coming out of the wall.

'Peter,' Maggi whispered. 'What's that?'

'The plumbing,' he told her, putting his ear next to the wall.

'Oh wonderful,' Maggi said. 'The cell even has lousy plumbing. That, in its way, is the final straw!'

'Quiet for a second,' Peter said, still listening. He pulled a ballpoint out of his shirt pocket, looked vainly around, and then settled for the cuff of his sleeve. While he scribbled, Maggi looked on, holding her breath, like the witness to a magical incantation who is afraid to stir because it might somehow break the spell.

After a few minutes, the pinging stopped. Peter took a deep breath and paused to read what he had written. Maggi looked at the mutilated cuff and tried to make out what the letters were. After a second, she oriented herself to the Carthage style of block capitals, and was able to read them.

ANYONE HEAR ME IF YOU
UNDERSTAND THIS PLEASE
ANSWER PLEASE

'Peter! Who is it? What kind of message is that tapping — some sort of Morse code? Is it another prisoner? What do you think he wants?'

'Please,' Peter said. 'One thing at a time. Let me answer him first; then we'll see if we can find out the rest.' He picked up one of the soup spoons and looked for a place to bang out his reply. The small sink in the corner of the cell had a good, substantial-looking drainpipe, so he went over and tried hitting it. It gave a good, solid clunk, but the sound damped itself out before it had left the cell. 'A problem,' he said. 'It looks like we might have only one-way communication here. The only other things I can see to bang on are the bars in the door; they probably won't make any noise, and if they do, all it will accomplish will be to bring the guard.'

'Maybe,' Maggi suggested, 'since the sound came from this wall, there's something in the wall you can use to send it back.'

'That's my girl,' Peter said, squatting down by the wall to examine it. 'It's probably some old rusted-out drainpipe that's been cemented over at this end, but . . . no, by God, here it is!' He dropped flat to the floor and scraped away at something in the corner. 'It's just a rusted-out hole now — must have had a drainpipe or something in it once. Ah! Here's the end of the pipe. Now, let's see if there's enough unrusted metal to bang on.' He took the spoon and banged it around in the small hole. After a few seconds, he was rewarded by hearing a solid plicking sound. 'Success. Our intercom seems to be working. Now, let's see if we have the right pipe.'

Plick, Plick. Plick. Plick. Plick . . . Plick.

Peter banged away with the spoon industriously for a minute, then paused to wait for an answer.

Ping. Ping . . . The answer came.

'That's it,' Peter said, starting to write on his cuff. 'Now let's find out who we're talking to.'

'Wait a minute,' Maggi said, clutching Peter's arm. 'Listen here, by the door.'

Peter went over to the door. From somewhere down the hall, slight clinking and thunking noises were originating. 'It sounds like they're coming to get me,' he whispered to Maggi. 'Listen fast — I don't have much time. They're going to take me away to finish the questioning.

While I'm gone, you've got to find out who's at the other end of that pipe — he might be our key out of this place.'

'That's fine,' Maggi said, nodding at him solemnly. 'I can see that. But you'll have to tell me what all that banging means if I'm going to use it to talk to anyone.'

'Right,' Peter said, ripping off his left cuff. 'It's called the prisoner's code, and I wrote it here. It's very simple.' He handed the scrap of fabric to Maggi, and she saw that it contained a kind of chart made up of the letters of the alphabet in a five-by-five square:

	1	2	3	4	5
1	A	B	C	D	E
2	F	G	H	I/J	K
3	L	M	N	O	P
4	Q	R	S	T	U
5	V	W	X	Y	Z

'How does it work?' Maggi asked.

'The number of raps establishes the letter by row and then column,' Peter told her. 'For example, one-one would be row one, column one, or A. One-three would be row one, column three, or C. Four-five would be the letter U. The word 'love' in prisoner's code is three-one, three-four, five-one, one-five. Do you see?'

'I think so,' Maggi said. 'Why are the I and the J together?'

'Two letters have to be put together to make it a perfect five-by-five square, and the I and the J are the letters by ancient custom. I think it somehow dates back to Latin usage.'

'I'll take your word for it,' Maggi said, staring doubtfully at the chart. 'If I can manage to work this thing, what do you want me to find out from whoever is banging at us?'

'Everything you can,' Peter told her. 'Who he is, what he's doing here — like that. And I'm sure you can do it. I have the utmost confidence in you. You do a good job at this, Miss Blaine, and you might be next in line for the vice-presidency of the internal communications section.'

'Good-o,' Maggi said. 'Do I get a gold watch?'

'I'll personally see that you get what's coming to you,' Peter assured her. 'Now, here they come. See what you can find out while I'm gone.' He kissed her on the forehead.

'Peter!' Maggi choked out his name, trying hard not to show any emotion and almost succeeding. She grabbed him and pressed her lips to his, both of her arms locked around his neck so tightly he could hardly breathe. After a long moment, she let go. 'Peter. Take care of yourself.'

'Don't worry about me,' Peter said. 'You're the one with the job for today. While I'm relaxing and answering a few simple questions, you'll be up here pounding away at a small hole in the wall with a soup spoon.' He kissed her, gently but firmly.

The cell door opened, and the giant was standing there with a smaller friend. Peter left between them, and they closed the door and started down the hall with him.

12745 Removal apparatus test procedure
12746 Modular Group Five (5).

15

On the balcony overlooking the great central chamber, the Marquis Chang Hu strode back and forth, tirelessly directing the ordered frenzy below. The great cubes of computer sections were scattered on the chamber floor like a child's blocks, connected by the sausage-cable axons that made them man's closest artificial approximation to thought — an approximation that, in many ways, was superior to the original.

Like ants in a nest — or perhaps, more closely, like ancient priests before the altar of a vengeful god — the brown-clad monks serviced, fed, taught, abluted, directed, tested, repaired, appeased and programmed the massive components of the electronic brain known as the Mind of Chang Hu. Like the high priest and oracle, on the balcony above, Chang Hu collected and read the computer output, directing his minions in accord with the wisdom of his Mind.

On the main floor, a small amber bulb lit on the center panel of one control board, and a line of type spewed out of the computer's maw. The brown-robed tech at that board flipped two switches and pushed a button.

The blinking light on the master control board drew Chang Hu over to the repeater, where he read the output for himself. He ripped the page and handed it to the small monk who trotted behind him as he paced. The monk did his best to uncrumple it, and clipped it into a large green daybook he carried between folded arms next to his chest.

The Marquis picked up a microphone. 'Attention all personnel! Final tests of the removal apparatus for projects Alpha and Omega are now to be made in the miniature pit. Prepare the models!'

Across one side of the central chamber, a double-line of monks dog-trotted vigorously, their robes flapping about them as their sandaled feet beat in double-time along the flagstone floor. They formed themselves on the two long sides of a large, raised section of the floor, picked it up, and walked off with it, revealing a deep pit beneath.

Two technicians took up positions by the wall next to the pit. 'Activate!' One of the technicians flicked a switch set into the wall. The stone front dropped into the floor, revealing racked panels of electronic controls. The two technicians took their places at the controls and the one on the left rotated a large wheel. From the pit, concealed lighting came on, and slowly grew brighter as the wheel turned.

The Marquis strode over to the side of the balcony above the pit and looked down. 'Begin!'

A droning throb came from the depths of the pit, gradually filling the air. Slowly, ponderously, a six-foot-long, fat, gray, cigar-shaped object rose out of the pit. It hovered in the air for a minute, about three feet off the ground, then rose to a height of twenty feet — parallel with the Marquis on his balcony.

The Marquis stared speculatively at the miniature Zeppelin, which ignored him majestically from twelve feet away. 'Give the Mind complete control,' he ordered. A monk flipped a switch.

'I HAVE ASSUMED CONTROL,' the Mind of Chang Hu announced over the loudspeakers in a metallic voice. 'EVASIVE MANEUVERS ARE BEGINNING.'

The ship darted back and forth and from side to side in an intricate series of sharp-angle turns that carried it gradually across the room. 'THESE MOTIONS,' the machine announced, 'EACH OF TWO POINT FIVE SECONDS' DURATION, ARE BASED ON A TABLE OF RANDOM NUMBERS SO THAT, WHILE THE OVERALL DIRECTION REMAINS CONSTANT, THE SPECIFIC DIRECTION AT ANY GIVEN INSTANT CANNOT BE PREDICTED BY FIRE CONTROL ANTI-AIRCRAFT RADAR.'

Chang Hu turned to the monk beside him. 'The machine not only controls the escape ship,' he commented, 'it even explains what it's doing. That is much. That is indeed much. That is, perhaps, too much. I must think on it.'

A white-smocked assistant approached Chang Hu with the proper deference, hands clasped in front of him, head bobbing with every step. 'Doctor, Peter Carthage is ready for the questioning chamber.'

'So?' Chang Hu froze for a moment and then turned to his assistant. 'Continue with the trial, and report to me any difficulties — especially with the submarine.'

'Of course, Excellency.'

'Then I go.'

★ ★ ★

Peter was stretched out, unconscious, on a table with three white-coats working over him when Chang Hu entered the chamber. 'Is he ready?' the ancient Manchu asked, bending over the still form and peering with interest into Peter's face.

'The last two minutes, Excellency. We thought you'd like to watch the final preparations.'

'Ah! Yessss,' he hissed his approval.

The white-coats continued their preparation: shaving little patches on Peter's head to attach electrodes; setting in place the apparatus to record blood pressure, respiration, heartbeat, and skin conductivity.

'Now?' Chang Hu asked.

'Now,' the chief white-coat agreed. He checked some of the readings on the bank of instruments that were now attached to Peter, and then gave him a carefully measured injection. 'In about three minutes he should be in half-sleep, and ready for interrogation.'

'Fine. Wheel him into the chamber.' The extra-long hospital table carrying Peter and the bank of instruments was taken into the next room. Special output leads from the instruments were plugged into a remote board that was the only furniture in the gray-painted, featureless room. The technicians left the room, leaving Chang Hu and the unconscious Peter alone — except for the blinking amber eyes of the remote board that was an extension of the Mind of Chang Hu.

The Marquis sat, arms folded, in a metal chair in a far corner of the room, and stared with unbroken concentration at the still tableau before him.

After a time, prompted perhaps by a change in blood pressure or in the alpha waves of Peter's brain, the speaker grille mounted above the remote board broke into sound. 'CARTHAGE, OLD FRIEND. I SIT HERE BEFORE YOU AT MY USUAL DESK READY TO RECEIVE YOUR REPORT. I AM DOCTOR STEADMAN, THE OLD MAN. I SIT HERE BEHIND MY DESK AND YOU WILL REPORT TO ME. YOU WILL REPORT TO ME. YOU WILL SEE ME SITTING HERE BEHIND MY DESK AND YOU WILL REPORT TO ME. I AM DR. STEADMAN, YOUR BOSS, AND YOU WILL REPORT TO ME. I AM SITTING HERE SMOKING MY OLD PIPE. MISS COW, MY SECRETARY, IS BRINGING IN SOME TEA FOR US WHILE YOU REPORT TO ME. I MUST KNOW WHAT YOU ARE DOING IN ALBA. YOU WILL REPORT TO ME . . . '

Peter stirred and shook his head, as if to clear it, without trying to get up from the table — or, indeed, seeming to realize that he was on a table. It would have been hard to say whether he was conscious or not. He made several sounds that might have been an attempt at speech, but were too indistinct to tell.

'YOU MUST ANSWER ME. YOU MUST TALK TO ME. I AM DOCTOR STEAD-MAN. HELLO, PETER CARTHAGE. SIT DOWN. HAVE A CUP OF TEA. REPORT. REPORT.'

Peter opened his eyes. Things were fuzzy and indistinct for some reason, but he knew where he was. He was in Doctor Steadman's office, sitting on one side of the big mahogany desk. He was also — some-where — it wasn't clear — somewhere else — but he couldn't make that out right now. He'd worry about that later. There was something else — something he was supposed to report on — but he didn't know what it was. 'Wha . . . what . . . what is it?'

'I AM DOCTOR STEADMAN. YOU MUST TALK TO ME. HELLO PETER CARTHAGE. IT IS GOOD TO SEE YOU AGAIN. IT IS GOOD TO HAVE YOU HERE IN MY OFFICE. I SIT HERE ACROSS THE TABLE FROM YOU, WITH MY PIPE IN MY MOUTH, TALKING

211

TO YOU JUST AS WE HAVE SO MANY TIMES BEFORE.'

There was a strangeness about the whole situation. Peter felt almost as if he was in a dream — as if some stranger were softly whispering to him. But this wasn't so. The only person in the room was Doctor Steadman, and he was just speaking normally. He had promised Peter a cup of tea — the tea that was such a tradition in the Old Man's office that it had become something of a joke. He remembered telling someone (who?) about it only the other day. When was it? Where was the tea? 'Where's the tea?'

'HERE IS THE TEA NOW. THANK YOU, MISS COW, FOR THE TEA. HERE IS YOUR CUP, PETER. JUST PUT IT DOWN THERE. NOW LET US TALK. I AM DOCTOR STEADMAN AND YOU MUST REPORT TO ME. WHAT HAVE YOU TO REPORT?'

'Thank you for the tea.'

'I AM GLAD YOU LIKE IT. YOU ARE WELCOME. NOW LET US TALK ABOUT YOUR REPORT. TELL ME ABOUT THE SITUATION IN ALBA.'

'Alba? What can I tell you? I've been in . . . I've been . . . that is, I'm . . . ' Peter tried to figure out what he was thinking. Something about being captured. How had he gotten away? He couldn't remember.

'JUST THINK ABOUT WHAT HAP-PENED IN ALBA. JUST THAT TIME. TELL ME ABOUT JUST THAT TIME. FIFTY CUBIC CENTIMETERS OF BETA SOLUTION. WHAT HAPPENED IN ALBA?'

What was that about some solution? Peter tried to concentrate on it, but couldn't. Doctor Steadman's office was starting to get hazy and more dreamlike, and Peter knew there was something wrong. He felt a sharp bite on his arm, and the voice of Doctor Steadman came back, reassuringly.

'I AM DOCTOR STEADMAN. YOU WILL TALK TO ME. YOU WILL REPORT TO ME ON THE SITUATION IN ALBA. I AM DOCTOR STEADMAN.'

Peter's doubts receded. He was again securely sitting in Doctor Steadman's office, talking to the Old Man. Everything became clear. 'What do you want to know about the situation in Alba?' he asked.

'DO YOU KNOW WHAT IS HAP-PENING THERE? WHAT HAVE YOU FOUND OUT ABOUT THE TWO GROUPS OPERATING THERE? I AM DOCTOR STEADMAN; YOU MUST TELL ME WHAT YOU KNOW.'

'Well,' Peter said, relaxing in his chair and staring across at the familiar, friendly face of Doctor Steadman, 'we haven't really found out too much. We know there are two groups operating there, and we have reason to suspect they're related somehow, but we have no idea of how.'

'THE TWO GROUPS ARE RELATED. YOU ARE SURE OF THIS?'

'Reasonably.' Peter looked around for his tea, but couldn't seem to find it.

'WHAT SORT OF PROOF HAVE YOU? WHAT SORT OF INFORMATION HAVE YOU?'

'There's no real proof. The only infor-mation we have is from that man Smith, and his story about the Marquis Chang Hu.'

'MISTER SMITH?'

'Yes. It was in the report.'

'TELL ME AGAIN.'

Peter settled down to talk to Doctor Steadman. The conversation lasted for some time. Every once in a while, things would get vague. But something would bite his arm and it would clear up again. Peter talked and talked.

As he talked, he got weaker and weaker, but he didn't notice that. He wasn't supposed to. He answered questions, smiled and chatted to the speaker grille mounted above the blinking lights. The pauses between his words got longer, and his voice got weaker, but he kept talking. Finally, he stopped and his eyes closed.

'THANK YOU, PETER CARTHAGE. YOU HAVE BEEN MOST HELPFUL. I AM DONE WITH YOU.'

From the corner he had been listening in, Chang Hu got up. 'Bah! And I am through with this whole idea. After all that, he didn't know a damn thing.' Chang pushed a button, and three of the white-coats returned.

'What shall we do with him, Excellency?' the lead white-coat asked, doing a ceremonial kowtow on the hard-wood floor.

'I don't care. Get rid of him. Throw him away. No — wait a minute. Save him; put him back in his cell. He still has some more to tell us about War, Incorporated, when I have time for him.'

'Yes, Excellency.' The white-coats detached the tubes and wires from Peter and wheeled his unconscious body out of the room.

16

Maggi stopped beating on the pipe when she heard them bringing Peter back to the cell. She stood in the corner when the door opened, trying to look guileless and bored. Then she saw Peter, carried like a flour sack between two white-coated stevedores, and her poise disappeared.

'Peter!' she yelled. 'What have they done? What's wrong?' The leather-jacketed giant stepped between her and the men carrying Peter. She tried to push her way past him and, when he wouldn't move, started beating against his chest. She wasn't a small girl, and the rigors of dancing kept her fairly strong, but her opponent didn't even seem to notice her. After a few seconds she slumped down on the door, sobbing.

'*Nosila!*' the giant directed. The white-coats put Peter down on the sleeping-shelf that ran across the back of the cell, and then hurriedly left. The giant looked down at Maggi, taking notice of her for the first time. 'He sleep,' the giant said. 'He be okay.' With that assurance, he turned around and left, slamming the wooden door firmly behind him.

Maggi got up, and seemed to be surprised to find that she was crying. Standing straight and tall, she closed her eyes and tensed all her muscles, pulling herself together physically and mentally. When she opened her eyes again, she had stopped crying and had regained control of her emotions. 'Now is not the time,' she told herself. 'Peter needs me, and I'm not going to be emotional.'

She went over to Peter and tried to wake him, but he wouldn't stir. His heartbeat and breathing seemed to be normal, but his sleep was too deep to pull out of. Maggi made him as comfortable as she could on the stone shelf, wrapping up his jacket and putting it under his head, and then sat beside him staring down at him for some sign of motion. For a long time neither of them moved.

'Pral tissen,' Peter suddenly cried, opening his eyes and staring at the ceiling.

'What, darling?' Maggi asked, stroking his face. 'What did you say?'

'Doctor Steadman . . . thank you . . . loom . . . tea . . . everything's fading out . . . ' Peter sat up. 'Your desk!' he screamed. 'It has eyes!' Then he collapsed back down on the shelf.

It was two more hours before Peter moved again. This time he slowly opened his eyes and looked around. 'Hello,' he said. 'Have I been here long?'

Maggi smiled weakly. 'Hello, darling. You weren't here at all until just now. It's good to have you back.'

'Yes,' Peter agreed. 'It's good to be back — I think. My memory of the past little while seems to be spotty. How long has it been?'

'They took you out of here this morning. It's now night, and you've been back three hours, so you've been gone all day. How long did you think it was?'

Peter tried to sit up, swinging his legs over the edge of the shelf, then thought better of it and lay back down. 'I'm dizzy,' he said. 'I'd better just lie here for a while. I have no objective idea of how much

219

time has passed; except, of course, what you just told me. Subjectively, it feels in some ways like weeks, and yet somehow like not more than a few minutes.'

'Where were you? What did they do to you?'

'I . . . That's funny, I'm not sure. I have a funny memory — but that's impossible.'

'What?'

'Let me think about it for a while and try to sort it out. I have a memory of doing something that I'm sure is impossible. I don't suppose there's anything to eat in here.'

'They brought the food around about an hour ago — I've saved your bowl.' Maggi brought it over and wiped the spoon on her skirt. 'It's pretty good. Open your mouth.'

'I'll do that myself,' Peter said. 'Wait a second until I sit up.' Maggi obediently moved aside while Peter tried to do so. After a few seconds, he gave up and collapsed back down.

'Now then,' she said, moving back to him and filling the spoon, 'open your mouth.'

After eating the whole bowl of rice and

vegetables, Peter fell into a sound, but normal, sleep. Maggi, who hadn't realized how tired she was, slept beside him.

'Hello again.'

Maggi opened her eyes.

'Sleep well?' Peter was up, recovered, cheerful, and had been doing something by the far wall.

'The sleep I slept was the sleep of the just,' Maggi said. 'How are you this morning?'

'Just about recovered. I've figured out what they did to me, so the mental confusion is disappearing. I'm getting on about the job of getting us out of here.'

Maggi sat up. 'I understand hard mattresses are good for your back, but this is carrying things too far,' she said, twisting her slender body around to get the stiffness out. 'Have you figured out how to get us out of here? Do you remember what they did to you?'

'Maybe. Yes.'

'Maybe yes?'

'No. Maybe — that's the answer to your first question. Yes is the answer to your second.'

'Oh. I forget what order I asked in. Which is maybe, and which is yes?'

'Maybe I can get us out of here. Yes, I remember what they did to me.'

'What did they do?'

'It was a form of drug-induced hypnotism. The interesting thing was that they used a machine to ask the questions and monitor my reactions.'

'A machine?'

'Some sort of computer.'

'How did it hypnotize you?'

'I was given a drug that put me to sleep, then I was hypnotized into believing I was in Doctor Steadman's office . . . '

'Who's Doctor Steadman?'

'My boss. Then the machine asked me a lot of questions, and I thought Doctor Steadman was asking, so I answered. They kept giving me more of the drug every time I started coming out of it.'

'That's very nasty. And they must have given you an awful lot of whatever it was to keep you knocked out so long.'

'I got a good night's sleep,' Peter agreed.

'What are we going to do now?' Maggi asked. 'How are we going to get out of here?'

'I'm working on it,' Peter said. 'I've been talking to your Chinese friend while you slept — if talking is the right word — trying to work something out. So far, we've had a couple of wild ideas, but nothing constructive.'

'My Chinese friend? Oh, you mean Hong, our fellow-prisoner at the other end of the rusty water pipe. Yes, we had a long, er, talk after you left yesterday. I got pretty good with the prisoner's code. What does he say this morning?'

'He says good morning, he hopes I'm in good health, and he wonders if we can help each other get out of here. Me, I also wonder. We also decided that he's about at the other end of the corridor, since if he yells real loud I can just about hear him. The idea now is to exchange information, and see if one of us knows something that will help the other figure a way out of here.'

Maggi rested her chin on her two fists and sighed. 'There was a cartoon in — I think — *The New Yorker* years ago that I clipped out and pasted on the wall above my work table. I think it was prophetic.'

'What was it?' Peter asked.

'Two men chained to a wall. They've obviously been there for some time. One of them is leaning over, as much as he can, toward the other. The caption is: 'Now, here's my plan . . . ''

'Very funny,' Peter said. 'I think I'll continue my communication with Mister Hong.'

'Is there anything I can do?' Maggi asked.

'Smile and hope,' Peter instructed her. 'If I think of anything more useful, I'll tell you.' He picked up the spoon he was using to bang out the code on the water pipe and squatted in the corner of the cell.

There was a scratching sound from outside the door. Peter turned, sliding the spoon up his sleeve, and sat up. The door swung open, revealing a small, dirty man in the badly-fitting costume of a monk. One of his eyes was partially closed by a long scar that ran diagonally across his face and curled under his chin. The other eye was bloodshot and stared out across the bridge of his nose.

'Mister Carthage?' he asked, peering into the cell.

Maggi retreated to the far corner, leaving Peter to deal with their visitor.

'What is it?' Peter asked.

'If you wish to transmit messages by banging on a pipe with a spoon, you'll have to be more careful to avoid being heard. The sound carries clearly out to the hall.' The grimy monk entered the cell and swung the door closed behind him.

Peter tensed himself. This might be his chance. The monk seemed to be alone and was out of sight of the hall. If he could knock the man out without giving him a chance to cry out, then . . .

'Who are you talking to, anyway?' The man peered through the Judas window back out into the hall, and Peter took a step toward him, clenching the spoon tightly in his fist. The handle of a spoon can be thrust upward through the throat in such a way that the larynx is separated from the head instantly, and the victim is unable to make a sound during the four or five seconds it takes him to die. When he turned back to the room, and his throat was exposed . . .

'I didn't expect you to be ecstatic, but you can at least be glad to see me,' the man said, turning. 'After all, I'm probably your only chance to get out of here.'

'What's that?' Peter pulled the spoon out of his sleeve and readied it behind his back.

'You don't recognize me?'

'No,' Peter admitted, tensing the spoon. 'Lift your head a bit so I can see you better.'

The monk put his head in his hands and his shoulders shook. Peter couldn't decide whether he was crying or laughing. Ten seconds later, he lifted his head. 'Recognize me now?'

The scar was gone, part of the nose was gone, and the eyes were open and straight. The face now looked normal.

'Mister Smith!'

'That's right, but keep your voice down.' Smith stretched and stood up. He now looked several inches taller. 'Ah, this is a relief. I am glad to stretch myself. It's no joke when a tall man has to take a foot off his stature for several hours on end.'

Maggi took a step forward, her eyes wide. 'Do you know this man? What's happened to his face?'

'Maggi, this is Mister Smith. I've told you about him. He's on our side. Don't ask me what he's doing here, because I have no idea.'

'My face?' Smith smiled. 'I try to keep it as flexible as my height.'

'What are you doing here?' Peter asked.

'I've been here for some time,' Smith said. 'I promised you more information, and I came here to get it. The only trouble is, now that I'm here, I can't get out.'

'You're not a prisoner too?'

'No, I'm a Lascar assistant of the good Doctor Chang Hu. One of the few non-Chinese monks in this Albanian monastery.'

'What's a Lascar?' Maggi asked.

'And why can't you leave?' Peter asked.

'Lascar, my dear, is an Indian dialect word meaning seaman, or dock worker. It has, in current usage, come to mean an evil or scurrilous person, particularly one from the East. The Marquis has many helpers who can best be described by this term. I can't leave because in the disguise I have adopted I have no excuse to go outside of the monastery grounds, and any attempt to would meet with instant suspicion from the guards.'

'Couldn't you get away from the guards?'

'Certainly I could. But then I couldn't come back. No, my main problem is simply that I haven't yet gathered all of the information that I came for. Once I have discovered the whole plan, I will remove myself from these surroundings as rapidly as possible. My present problem is to find a way to get you out of here. And it must be done quickly.'

'I'm glad you showed up,' Peter said. 'Is there a particular need for haste in getting us out of here now?'

Mister Smith shrugged. 'That depends on your point of view,' he said. 'Chang Hu intends to question you once more later in the week, and then dispose of you.

If you want to wait around for that, I have no objection. On the other hand, if you'd like to leave . . . '

'You've convinced me,' Peter said. 'How do we get out of here?'

'That's the problem. I don't know whether you do get out of here or not.'

'Swell.'

'Mister Smith,' Maggi said, 'you have to get us away from here! Do you know what they were doing to Peter?'

'Yes,' Smith said, 'I know.'

'Well, can you get us away from here or not?'

'I can get you out of here — that is, this cell — but I don't know if I can get you away from the monastery. The important thing is that I can put you somewhere Chang Hu can't find you.'

'In this position, I'll be grateful for whatever help you can be; but why can't you get us out of the monastery?'

'The operation is about to begin. Security precautions are particularly high right now. If I can hide you for a few days here, then getting you out will be much easier. Besides, by that time they'll have stopped looking for you.'

'Very convincing,' Peter said. 'Have you a place to hide us?'

'I think so. It'll be a bit of trouble getting you there, but once there, you'll be safe.'

'Do you know what the operation they're preparing for is yet?'

'I have a general idea. I hope to know better within a short time.'

'Mister Smith,' Maggi asked, 'can you do anything for Hong?'

'Hong?'

'The gentleman I was tapping to when you came in,' Peter explained. 'Hong pi-Hing, a representative of the government of the People's Republic of China. He's a prisoner here too. I wasn't able to get his whole story, but he might be able to help us.'

'Where is he?'

'I think he's in the last cell in this corridor,' Peter said.

'Wait here, I'll find out.'

'We have nowhere to go.'

'That's true,' Smith admitted. Then he left the cell, closing the door behind him.

'What a strange man,' Maggi said. 'He moves with such short, choppy motions. And he has the strangest look in his eyes. Do you know him well?'

'I've had several long talks with him,' Peter said. 'For a while I thought he had a fixation on one idea, but everything he said seems to be turning out true, so I don't know.'

'A man can be a monomaniac on one idea even if it's true,' Maggi said.

'That's right,' Peter said. 'Also, an idea fixation can be very useful. The best guard, all other things being equal, is the man who thinks he's going to be attacked.'

The cell door opened. 'Here's your man,' Smith said, escorting a round-looking Chinese individual dressed in mattress-ticking jacket and pants.

'My pleasure,' the man said, bowing slightly. 'I feel that I already know the two of you well. I am Hong pi-Hing.'

'It's good to see you, Mister Hong. I'm Peter Carthage, and this is Miss Maggi Blaire.'

'Ah, yes.' Hong took Maggi's hand in a

courtly gesture and pressed it to his lips. 'The charming lady with whom I spent most of yesterday conversing.'

'Before we go on with this,' Smith interrupted, 'I'd like to ask Mister Hong a few questions.' He carefully pulled the cell door closed and stood with his back to it, legs balanced wide apart.

'But, of course,' Hong said, turning to face Smith, hands clasped carefully together across his chest. 'What is it that you wish to know?'

'*Muy yang*,' said Mister Smith. '*Foy than di yappa lichi* . . . ' His voice slid across the five tones of Mandarin like a singer doing complex half-tone scales. Hong replied in the same language, and the two of them stood there, three feet apart from each other, singing this complex half-tonal duet for some time.

'What are they talking about?' Maggi whispered to Peter.

'Chinese isn't one of my accomplishments,' Peter told her. 'Wait until they're done. Smith must have something in mind.'

'If Hong is really Chinese, why did he

talk to us in English?' Maggi asked.

'As a matter of fact, I asked him that when we were tapping back and forth this morning. He heard me talking to the guard when they took me down that corridor. That's how he knew he had someone to try to communicate with, and what language to try in.'

'All right,' Smith said, switching suddenly back to English, 'let's figure out how to get you out of here.'

'Fine,' Peter said. 'What was all that about?'

'Well,' Smith said, 'there was the chance — slight, I'll admit — that Mister Hong was a plant. The Marquis Chang Hu is a subtle man. I was trying to lessen the chance.'

'Did you?' Peter asked.

'I believe that Mister Hong is or was a representative of the government of the People's Republic of China fairly recently. There is, I admit, the chance that he has been subverted and is now working for the Marquis, but the risk is slight and the chance is worth it.'

'I don't understand,' Maggi said. 'You

mean that Chang Hu isn't an agent of Communist China?'

'If there's one thing I'm sure of,' Smith said, 'it's that the Marquis Chang Hu isn't now, and has never been, the agent of any government or organization. He is totally ruthless and completely self-oriented, a monomaniac who would cheerfully destroy the world if there was any profit in it for him. No, believe me, he works alone, and all his agents work only for him.'

'That's pretty clear,' Peter said. 'While we three, hiding in this cell, work against him.' He turned to Hong. 'What will the official Chinese attitude toward this be? I mean, how far will you help us?'

'That, I am afraid, at the present time is two separate questions. The official attitude of the Party would be that anyone who claims to be a direct descendant of the Manchu princes is a liar, a myth, or part of a capitalistic plot. Also, it seems from the questioning I've had here that the Marquis must have agents in high places in the People's government, or in the Party itself.'

Maggi asked, 'How can you judge that? *He* was questioning *you.*'

'That's so,' Hong admitted. 'I judge by the questions he asked. Knowing the right questions to ask can indicate a high degree of prior knowledge. Also, his men have successfully been masquerading as representatives of the People's Government here. It's only because of one message, which evidently got through by mistake, that I was sent here; and they knew I was coming. They were waiting for me.

'As to your other question: if I were to go back home now, after having failed in my mission and been captured, I'd be lucky to just be retired. I could just as easily be tried as a traitor and shot. Therefore, I believe that it's time for a mandatory retirement on my part. Perhaps to the United States or Great Britain. I would endeavor to pay my way and provide for my retirement fund out of certain stored-up bits of — ah — merchandise.' Hong looked around. 'Well, is anyone interested?'

'Wait until we get out of here,' Peter

told him. 'I work for a private organization that might be able to use your services. If not, I can put you in touch with those who can.'

'Fine,' Hong said, extending his hand. 'I hereby formally defect.'

'Like an oral contract,' Peter said, taking and shaking Hong's hand. 'You're on.'

Smith, who had been pacing the floor with his hand rubbing his chin while this conversation went on, stopped pacing and pointed a finger at Hong. 'I believe I have it!' he stated.

Hong took a step backward. 'What do you have?' he asked.

'The answer. The solution.'

'That is fine,' Hong agreed. 'What was the problem?'

'Now listen,' Smith said, lowering his voice, 'here's what we're going to do . . . ' He stopped and darted over to the Judas window, peering out into the hall for a long moment before returning to the group. It reminded Peter of a quarterback pausing to take one last good look at the opposition's lineup before going into the huddle. 'Now,' Smith said, 'here's my plan.'

They gathered around Smith as he lowered his voice and started detailing his scheme. 'We don't have much time,' he said. 'First we have to get you and Miss Blaire to my hiding place, where you'll both be safe for a couple of days.'

'What about Mister Hong?' Maggi asked. Hong looked interested in the answer.

'Mister Hong is the only one of us that stands a chance of getting out of here now. So that's what we'll do. I can get Hong as far as the road away from here; after that, he's on his own.' He turned to Hong. 'Do you think you can manage from there?'

Hong shrugged. 'I am happy that you can get me out of this place. I think that if I had as much as a half-hour head start I could probably get away. The only problem is, where would I go? I can think of no safe place that I could reach from here.'

'That's part of my idea,' Smith said. 'We're going to send you to Alba. It won't be easy to get there, but once you make it you'll be safe.'

'Where is Alba?' Hong asked.

'Directly north of here. It's the country that Chang Hu is planning to attack.'

'I know that. I just didn't know where it was located. How far away is it?'

'About eighty miles, over some of the worst roads in the world.'

'What do I do when I reach the border?'

'Get to the Alban border guards — you'll have to get past the Albanians somehow — and ask for the men from War, Incorporated. Once there, you'll tell them what you know.'

'Fine,' Hong agreed. 'What do I know?'

'Perhaps I should have said what I know. I'll tell you what I've found out since I've been here, and you pass it on.'

'Now I see. Very fine. Tell me.'

Smith went out to check the halls again, then came back and resumed his hearty whispering. 'We should have two hours, at least. Possibly between three and four. All right, I'll tell you what I've found out; then we'll start the exodus.

When you get to Alba, tell . . . ' He turned to Peter. 'Tell who?'

'Professor Perlemutter, I guess.'

'Yes. Tell Professor Perlemutter what Chang Hu is planning, and you will have repaid us for helping you escape.'

'It shall be done,' Hong said, writing PEARL MUTTER on the cuff of his shirt with a felt-tipped pen. 'If I am to become a capitalist, I should start paying my way. Now, what do I tell this Professor Mutter?'

'That's . . . oh, never mind,' Peter said. No sense in adding to the confusion.

'There are three events planned to happen simultaneously,' Smith explained. 'A raid on the casino, a hijacking of the paper mill, and an invasion by the Albanian Army. The last, the invasion, is to be a big scare to pull the police off the other two, and the Army is supposed to turn around and go home before it gets too serious.'

'Before it *gets too serious*?' Peter said. 'My God, Smith, Alba is under the protection of Italy, and the Italian armed forces will certainly come to Alba's assistance. Doesn't that maniac know that a thing like that could touch off a third world war?'

'I assume he does,' Smith said. 'But I also assume that he doesn't care. If World War III starts, Chang Hu would only have to wait for its ending to be in a much better position to continue his ultimate plan: the conquest of the world.'

'You can't be serious,' Maggi said. 'This is some sort of joke!'

'I assure you that I'm serious. Look around you,' Smith said, sweeping his thin arm around in a gesture that encompassed the stone cell and the entire monastery. 'Does this seem a joke? How do you think he succeeded in taking control of a monastery? I'll tell you: he murdered the real monks and had his men take their place. Is that the act, or even the concept, of a sane man? No, the Marquis Chang Hu is insane, but diabolically clever; twisted, but frighteningly powerful; ancient as these walls, but infinitely patient. He is capable of anything. Anything.' Smith shook his head slowly from side to side. 'The stories I could tell you . . . But, back to the business at hand.'

'Do you know when this is planned for?' Peter asked.

'No, I haven't been able to find that out. I know no more than that little bit. Those three things are planned, and for the near future. I would say within the next ten days, perhaps much sooner.'

'How has Chang Hu managed to convince the Albanian Army to assist him?' Peter asked.

'The Albanian Army thinks they're preparing war games near the Alban border. Only the commanders of the companies to be used for the incursion, all three of them men in Chang Hu's control, know of the actual plan. The others think it is some sort of demonstration for some high-ranking Chinese Communist officials who are to show up and watch. The Marquis will supply the officials.'

'How have the hijackers and the casino bandits planned to get away?' Peter asked.

'Another item of information that I don't have,' Smith said. 'Come along now, I'm going to have to get you out of here. Hong, you'll have to wait in your cell until I come back for you; it's the only place where you won't look suspicious if you're found by accident.'

'That makes sense,' Hong acknowledged. 'But I know I'm not going to believe you're coming back until you do. I won't ask you to hurry up, but . . . '

'I understand completely,' Smith assured him. 'Stone walls might not a prison make, but they do nicely as a substitute.'

'You said that Mister Hong is the only one of us you can get out of here right now,' Maggi said. 'Why is that?'

'Simply because he's Chinese. Well, come along. Don't make any noise at all, and do exactly what I tell you to. I'll use hand gestures.'

'Er, Mister Smith . . . ' Maggi began.

'What is it?'

'If you use hand gestures, you'd better go over them once before we start. I've never been very good at hand gestures. They didn't cover it in my high school.'

'Very well. These are the hand gestures I shall use, if called upon to do so,' Smith said, then proceeded to demonstrate them. 'Now, if that's clear, we can continue.'

'Very good. Very clear,' Maggi said. 'Let's go.'

They left the cell and tiptoed down the long corridor fronting the bank of cell doors. At the very last one in the row, Hong said, 'Goodbye and good luck,' pulled the door open, stepped inside, and slid it closed behind him.

Smith slid the bar into place on the outside, locking the cell. 'I'll be right along for you,' he told Hong. Then he gave Peter and Maggi the *Follow me* gesture, and trotted around the bend in the corridor.

They went around, down a short flight of stone steps, along a narrow hall, and into a small, square room with two doors. 'Wait here for me,' Smith told them, and went out the other door. They waited.

Time passed. Peter stood by the wall next to the far door and listened. Maggi silently leaned against him, and he wrapped his arm around her. She clung onto it and tried to smile. Footsteps approached the door and then receded away again. They didn't move. More footsteps, two pairs this time, approached the door and stopped on the other side. Two gruff male voices had a discussion outside the door in a language Peter didn't recognize. Peter let go of Maggi and kissed her on the forehead, then gently pushed her into the corner of the room. He took his belt off and wrapped it around his hand, allowing the heavy buckle to swing on about four inches of leather. The footsteps started again, and the voices went away without entering the room. Peter slowly let his breath out, and then realized that he'd been holding it.

Footsteps approached again, and Peter clenched his belt. The door opened and Smith came in. He stared at Peter. 'What on earth have you been up to?'

'People have been walking by the door. I thought they might come in,' Peter explained, buckling his belt back around his waist.

'I wouldn't have left you in a room that anybody was going to wander into,' Smith said testily. 'Here, put these on.' He handed a brown bundle to Peter, and one to Maggi.

'You and I know that,' Peter agreed,

'but did you tell them?' He shook his bundle out into its proper shape of baggy monk's robe, and wrapped the thing around him. It was heavy, it itched, and it smelled of sweat and garlic, but Peter decided it would do.

The one Maggi had on was too big for her. It enveloped her completely, and the bottom trailed along the floor. 'Pull it up,' Smith directed, 'and let some of it flap out around that rope tied around your middle.'

'Try not to let any of your leg show,' Peter added. 'That's a very un-monkish leg.'

While Maggi and Peter struggled to approximate the appearance of the grimy monks about them, Smith sat at a small table in one corner and busied himself with a mirror. After a few minutes, he looked up at them. The face that now peered out from the monk's cowl was the scarred, ugly one that had first greeted them in the cell. 'I think we're about ready to continue,' he said. And when he stood up, he was a foot shorter than when he sat down.

'Very impressive,' Peter said. 'Your disguise is artful.'

'The art of deception should usually be kept very simple,' Smith told him. 'A change of the shape of the nose, a darkening or lightening of the complexion, a new manner of walking: these should suffice. But when one is dealing with the Marquis, it is best to take no chances — or as few as possible, at any rate.' He put his finger to his lips. 'Now! No more talking. Follow me, walking in single file as though you know where you are going. If anyone attempts to talk to you, do not answer, but leave everything to me. If our disguise is penetrated our only hope will be to immediately silence anyone in sight or hearing. Failing to do that, we are dead!' With that cheery last word, he turned and led the way out of the room. Maggi followed and Peter took last position.

The hall they walked down joined a larger one after a few yards. They turned left and continued walking. More small halls joined the large one as they went along. It reminded Peter of rivers coming together as they neared the sea. Brown-clad men passed them, going the other way, and took no notice of them. It seemed to Peter that the trio looked like circus clowns and must be spotted at once, but no one that passed seemed to see anything unusual.

They reached the entrance to what seemed to be a large room. Smith stopped there and waited for the other two to catch up with him. 'One at a time,' he whispered. 'Straight across, by the wall. I'll be waiting at the far door.' He left.

After a suitable interval, Peter squeezed Maggi's shoulder. 'Okay, girl. Head out. I'll be right behind you.' Maggi started walking across the room, looking straight ahead, marching to the dirge of a different drummer. Monks passed on all sides of her, and they ignored her completely. Peter breathed a silent prayer of thanks to Loki, his patron god, and started across.

The chamber proved to be very large, and filled with computer equipment being nursed by squads of monks. The ceiling seemed high enough to hold banks of clouds below it. On the far side of the chamber, stretching the length of one wall, was a balcony on which paced one tall man. Peter thought that even from this distance he could make out the features of the Marquis Chang Hu.

Trying to appear as though he wasn't hurrying, Peter headed toward the door that Maggi was just passing through. Suddenly, a monk carrying a tray of file cards turned and took a step toward Peter. He found himself staring the monk right in the face, and it was one he recognized from the interrogation team the first day. Slowly, Peter saw recognition spread across the monk's homely face.

'Excuse me,' Peter said, and he jammed his stiffened fingers deep into the monk's neck right below the chin. The monk blanked and started to slide to the floor, his face turning bright red.

Peter took the tray of cards out of the monk's hands before they had a chance to spill, and set them on a table. Then he slid the unconscious man under the same table as quickly as he could, and stood up and started to walk away. He didn't look around to see if anyone had noticed; if he had been seen, the outcry would start within the next fraction of a second.

The hairs on the back of his neck prickled as he walked, but no one yelled. Then he was at the far door and into the stone corridor.

'What happened?' Smith whispered hoarsely.

'Someone recognized me, so I put him under a table. He should be good for a couple of hours if no one spots him.'

'Let us pray,' Smith commented. 'Come on.'

They continued down the corridor, turned into one of the side corridors, and then stopped in front of a closed wooden door. Smith took a large key from somewhere and unlocked it.

'Another cell?' Maggi asked softly.

'A staircase.' They entered, and Smith closed and locked the door behind them. 'Now we go up.' With Smith leading, they started climbing the old wooden stairs.

They climbed and climbed. 'Where are we?' Peter asked. 'I didn't know the building was this high.'

'Most of it isn't,' Smith told him. 'This is the tower.'

'Oh.'

'No windows?' Maggi complained. 'What good is a tower without windows?'

'The windows start nearer to the top,' Smith said.

Finally, after a long climb, they reached the first glass panes. A few minutes later, they came out into a small room that was circled by windows. 'The tower room,' Smith told them.

'So this is it,' Peter said, looking around.

'No, sorry. This isn't it,' Smith said.

'Where else can we go?' Peter asked.

'They occasionally come up here to watch the road,' Smith said. 'Not usually, but sometimes. However, they never go up there — ' He pointed toward the ceiling of the small room. ' — so that's where you're going.'

'The ceiling?' Maggi asked.

'The roof,' Smith told them. 'It's the only place I know you won't be found. And believe me, they'll be looking for you.'

'I believe you,' Peter said. 'How do we get up there?'

'Here, this way.' Smith slid a thin iron rod from his sleeve and inserted it into a crack in the wall. 'This wasn't designed to be so mysterious, but the original handle broke off. We now have a hidden door.' He twisted the rod. There was a sharp cracking sound overhead, and a section of the ceiling dropped downward on hinges, sending a rope ladder cascading into the room.

'The ladder is permanently attached to the trapdoor,' Smith told them. 'Just pull it up after you and close the trap.'

'Secure on the roof,' Peter said. 'Can anyone see us from below?'

'Not unless you peer over the edge. Even then, they probably wouldn't notice, but I don't advise it.'

'And they can't get at us unless they know about the little gizmo there,' Peter said, indicating the rod-and-crack door-knob.

'Not even then,' Smith told them. 'There are bolts on the other side of the trap that you can throw to keep it closed.

If anyone does try it, they'll probably think it's been rusted shut, and forget about it. I don't believe anyone else here knows about it in any case. I found it because I was specifically looking for a place to hide that even an organized search would probably miss, and I've had a lot of experience. I think you'll be perfectly safe up there until I can get you out. Cold, perhaps, but safe.'

'Have we anything to take up there besides these robes?' Maggi asked. 'Any blankets, or food? You said we're likely to be up there for a few days, and the nights on top of this mountain get pretty cold. I mean, I'm not complaining; it's better than the cell, and it's a step toward getting away from this place.'

'Of course,' Smith said. 'This is a pre-pared bolt-hole. I was getting it ready for myself in case of need. When I discovered that you were captured, I added some supplies for this eventuality. You'll find blankets and supplies up there. When I come to get you, I'll tap 'Rule Britannia' on the ceiling, and you let down the trap-door. You'd best go up now.'

They clambered up the rope, Peter first this time. When he was up, he turned to help Maggi through; then gave the victory sign to Smith, pulled up the rope, and closed the trapdoor. He rose and looked around. The roof of the tower was a twenty-by-twenty-foot square with a waist-high parapet. As soon as he stood up so that his body was above the parapet, a gale-force wind struck him in the chest, knocking him back down. It wasn't until then that he realized the thin, whistling sound that surrounded him came from air moving over the stone ledge: cold, high-speed air.

'Don't stand up,' he told Maggi.

'Why? What's the matter?'

'There's a hurricane going on up there. Where's Smith's stuff?'

'Over there, in that corner.'

'Good. Let's break it out and play house. We're going to be here for a while.'

17

Hong pi-Hing sat alone in his cell and meditated. He thought about his now-lost life in Peiping, his wife and his child, his job at the Ministry. He thought about his future life in the free world, his pending job as an 'intelligence analyst' — a polite term for *defector* — his new car. He thought about the Words of Chairman Mao, and how he'd never have to hear them again. He thought about everything except his impending escape. If he kept his mind off it, he might be able to avoid building up a barrier of fear. Fear against the idea of violent action. Fear of being hunted. Overwhelming, mind-paralyzing fear that could leave him crouched in a corner, unable to move. Fear that . . . no, mustn't think of that. Think about something else. Anything else. Even his wife. Think about . . .

The cell door opened. A small, twisted monk with a horrible scar stood in the doorway. Hong shrank back into his corner. He wasn't going to make it after all. He wasn't even going to get the chance to try to escape. Smith had taken too long, and they had come for him first.

'Well,' the small, twisted monk said in Smith's voice, 'I'm back. That didn't take too long, did it?'

'Mister Smith?' Hong asked.

'Who were you expecting? I . . . oh, I forgot about this — ' He indicated his face. ' — my disguise. Yes, it's me. Come on, we have to get you out of here. Put this on.' Smith passed Hong a white smock.

'A doctor's robe?' Hong asked, putting the thing on and tying it around him.

'Doctor's and chief technician's, yes. It's your passport out of here. The white robes are allowed to sign vehicles out if they have the proper authorization. No one else is. Consider yourself lucky; all the white-robes are Chinese. You ready?'

Hong nodded. 'What do I have to do?'

'Act as if you own the earth. Be nasty and imperious. Remember, we don't have the authorization that's required, so we'll have to fake you through. Can you drive a car?'

'Yes,' Hong said.

'Good. You'll have a driver, but you'll have to get rid of him and take over yourself. I forgot to ask you before: it's a lucky thing you *can* drive.'

'About that authorization,' Hong asked. 'Is it in Chinese?'

'Yes,' Smith said. 'But we don't have one.'

'Are the guards Chinese?'

'About half and half.'

'Then there's a good chance that the guard we see won't be able to read Chinese. Even if he is one of my countrymen, there's still a good chance. Can you get a piece of paper of the right general appearance?'

Smith clapped his hand to his forehead. 'Why didn't I think of that! Of course, you're probably right. At least, it's worth taking the chance. Come on, we'll take a slight detour.'

Smith led Hong through a maze of corridors and rooms, finally stopping in front of one. 'Clerical supply room,' he explained. 'Wait here.' He darted inside and was back out in under a minute. 'What a dunce,' he said. 'Under my nose all the time.' He waved a pad in the air. 'Blank forms; all we have to do is fill them in.'

Hong took the pad of forms and pulled his felt-tip pen out of his shirt pocket. He examined the paper for a while and then shrugged. 'A form is a form,' he said. With broad, precise strokes, he created Chinese characters on the top form. When he was done, he ripped it off and gave the pad back to Smith. 'All right. Let us make the attempt.'

As Smith led the way downstairs, around, up, over, and through, Hong was pleased to find that he was too involved to be frightened. The fright, he was sure, would come later, with either success or failure. Right now, all he had time for was the action of the moment: frowning importantly at half the people they passed, and ignoring distractedly the other half. Hong's years as a bureaucrat stood him in good stead now.

Smith stopped to one side of an open

door. 'The room through there is the vehicle dispatching office. I can't go in with you; it could blow the whole show. Good luck.'

Hong nodded calmly and walked past Smith into the office. Several youths sat in different levels of inattention on a bench beyond a low barrier. By the barrier sat an equally bored guard.

Hong looked at the scene with evident distaste. 'I don't expect anyone to get up and salute me,' he said acidly, 'but you could at least show some interest in my presence. I could be a spy, sent in to blow the place up. I could be an escaping prisoner trying to steal a car. I could be your boss!' By this time he had reached the barrier, and the men were starting to scramble to their feet.

'Yes, sir,' the guard said, just managing to stop himself from clicking his heels together. 'What can I do for you?'

'Luckily,' Hong told him, 'I am none of those things. I am merely a man wanting a car and driver.' He handed him the form. 'Preferably sometime in the near future.'

'Yes, sir,' the guard said. 'Of course, sir.' He put the form into a drawer without bothering to even try to read it, and called one of the loitering youths. 'Aihi, bring a limousine around; you're on call.'

The youth ran out of the room, and a few seconds later Hong heard the welcome sound of a car engine starting.

'Your car, sir,' the guard said, opening a gate in the barrier. Hong went through and out the far door. The 'limousine', he found, was a World War II U.S. Army Jeep. The driver had red welts in a ring around his neck from flea bites, and a youthful shock of hair that hung over his face like a sheepdog's and obscured his eyes. Hong sat well over on his side of the seat, and hoped that the driver could see the road.

The main monastery gate was opened without question as the Jeep approached it, and closed immediately when the vehicle had passed through.

'Not that it will matter for some time yet, sir,' the driver said, without — Hong praised God — taking his eyes off the incredibly convoluted road, 'but where do you wish me to take you?'

'Take me?' Hong repeated with an admirable show of nonchalance. 'Why, to the Alban border, of course.'

'Of course,' the driver repeated.

★ ★ ★

The most important thing in life, Professor Perlemutter stoutly maintained, was to never look surprised. 'And how did you cross the border?' he asked.

'That was no problem at all,' Hong told him. 'No Albanian border guard is going to refuse a request from a Chinese People's Republic official to inspect the border. I was escorted past the barrier by a major. When I reached the Alban side, I just patted him on the back, shook hands, and kept going.'

'Didn't he try to shoot?'

'He just stood there with his mouth open. For all I know, he is there yet.'

'Fantastic,' Professor Perlemutter said, managing not to look surprised. 'I suppose we have to believe you.'

'Mister Carthage told me that, for verification, I should tell you your first name. He says you'd know then that I came from him, because very few people know your first name. I think Sigismund is as nice as any other European name, but I suppose I'm no judge.'

'Yes, well,' Professor Sigismund Perlemutter said, 'that's what Peter would tell you; it sounds like him. Come with me, we'll have to talk to the others.'

18

The sun went out. There is really no other way to describe it. One moment it was sitting, carefully balanced, between the points of two mountains; the next, it had dunked itself into the western sea beyond the mountains, and all was black. Then a few dots appeared in the overhead dome. Then more and more, until the night sky sparkled with the light of countless suns and the starlight cast shadows across the deeper black.

The slight flicker of light-blue flame from the jellied-gasoline burner provided the only illumination, flickering beneath the pot of canned C-ration stew Maggi was heating for dinner. By this feeble light, Peter finished his housekeeping chores: blowing up the air mattress, unrolling the large sleeping bag, and setting the small shelter half-up as a triangular canvas protection against what wind managed to find its way below the stone wall.

'It's ready,' Maggi called softly. 'Come and get it.'

Peter came over to the little stove and took his can of stew. 'Primitive,' he said, squatting by Maggi and spooning some of the glutinous mass into his mouth, 'but acceptable. Barely, I might say, acceptable. Anyway, the vegetables are edible, even if sixty percent of the meat is gristle.'

'You can have some canned fruit salad for dessert; that seems pretty good. How do I put this thing out?' Maggi waved her hand over the burning can of jellied gas.

'Put the cover back on the can. Carefully, don't burn yourself — that stuff is very hot.'

Maggi took the cover gingerly between two fingers and approached the can with it. At the last moment, she dropped it on the open top. It landed square, but about a half-inch off-target, leaving the gas burning below the narrow opening. With a gesture of annoyance, she reached over to slide the top into place.

'Watch it!' Peter warned her. 'By now, that top will burn your hand. Here . . . ' He took his spoon and used it to move the cover. 'There. Now let it sit for a few minutes to cool down.'

'Sure thing. I'll let it sit all night. I have nowhere to put it, anyway.' They ate together in silence, enjoying each other's company and the brilliant display that the universe puts on every night for those far enough away from civilization to see it. After the meal, Maggi stacked the refuse in a carton that she had emptied for garbage.

'It's getting chilly,' she said, 'and the stars seem to be going out.'

'The sky seems to be getting a bit overcast,' Peter agreed. 'It's a shame. I like staring at stars.'

'I do too, for a while,' Maggi told him. 'But then I start feeling very small and insignificant, and I get scared; so I go inside.'

'It's a good idea for everyone to feel small and insignificant every once in a while. It should be a world-wide law that all public officials have to go outside and stare at the stars for a couple of hours at least once a month. It might help keep them human,' said Peter.

Maggi said, 'I see what you mean.' She stood up, and then quickly ducked again. 'That wind seems to be getting worse. I think it's about time for bed anyway.'

'I agree,' Peter said. 'It's been a long day. There's only one sleeping bag — I guess Smith was figuring on being up here alone — so you can have it.'

Maggi reached for his hand in the dark, and squeezed it. 'Nonsense! What are you going to do?'

'There are these monks' robes and things. I'll be okay.'

'That's silly. We can certainly share a sleeping bag. As I remember, most of them are big enough for two. We'll keep each other warm.'

That, Peter reflected, was one of the things he was worried about. Or not *worried*, exactly . . .

'If you were a woman,' Maggi told him, 'I wouldn't even want to share the same room with you. Women make lousy sleeping partners.'

'Only,' Peter told her, taking her firmly by the hand and guiding her over to the air mattress, 'for other women. Men usually prefer them.'

Maggi giggled. 'That's not exactly what I meant,' she said, 'but I see what you mean. And, speaking of what you mean, let's go to bed.' She pulled him down onto the mattress and ran her hand over his face, twining her fingers in his hair.

There is a natural law regarding the chemistry of such situations that says that if it's right, if the time is right, if the people are right for each other, and if the untold and unknowable other things that make for this chemistry are right, then suddenly speech becomes unnecessary. The things that one would have the other know are communicated by a touch, a look, a breath, and perhaps by some sense man has not yet named. And this is the magic and the rightness and the meaning as two people contemplate the act of becoming one.

★ ★ ★

The ship was sailing for wherever with all sails set, and the salt spray was hitting Peter in the face as he stood by the rail and watched the dock, which seemed to stay alongside of them as they sailed. The band, which consisted solely of drummers, was beating a steady rhythm from the dock to celebrate their coming or going. The thin red line of snare-drummers was like an exclamation mark, with the point being provided by a big kettle drum which the drunken band sergeant would occasionally play an out-of-beat roll on.

'Peter!'

The ship was developing a decided list to the side. The weight of the list, which was a giant roll of paper containing the names of all the drummers, rocked and tilted the boat, which was now a canoe . . .

'Peter. Wake up, darling. Please wake up.'

Peter opened one eye. He couldn't see anything at all. Maggi was shaking him gently and the drummers from his dream were still there. *That's funny*, he thought. He shook his head to try and clear some of the fuzz from his brain.

'You're awake!'

'Hello,' he said, for want of anything better. He felt dizzy, as though he were rolling gently from side to side.

'I'm sorry to wake you up,' Maggi whispered, 'but I'm afraid we're going to float away.'

'What?' Peter tried to sit up, but the zipped-up sleeping bag held him down. He unzipped it and put his hand out. It was up to the wrist in cold water. Now he was awake and understood what was happening.

'How long has it been raining?' he asked.

'I don't know,' Maggi told him. 'I just woke up a few minutes ago.'

The drumming noise of the rain hitting the canvas tent continued while Peter considered. 'We shouldn't be floating,' he said finally.

'I know,' Maggi agreed. 'But if we empty the air mattress, won't we get soaked?'

'I don't mean that,' Peter said. 'There should be a drain in the base of that wall somewhere. Probably at one of the corners.'

'It must be stuffed up,' Maggi said.

'I'll see.' Peter rolled out of the sleeping bag and stood up outside the tent. The rain was coming down at an angle, and it stung when it hit. 'Well, anyway, I'm awake now,' Peter yelled to Maggi. Prancing naked over to the nearest corner, he felt like he was in a gigantic shower. He reached down and examined the corner with his hands searching for an outlet. He had to examine three corners before he found what he was looking for: a round, four-inch-wide hole with a grating fixed over it. As Peter had suspected, over the years the grating had become clogged with dirt and debris. He scraped it clear, and felt the surge as the ankle-high water started to pour out.

'Mission accomplished,' he called. He went back to the tent and, crouching under the protective canvas, dried himself off the best he could with the soggy monk's robe before crawling back into the sleeping bag.

'You're freezing!' Maggi said, feeling his damp body. 'We can't let you get sick.' So saying, she snuggled up to him and wrapped herself around him, arms and legs entwined, and they both fell content-edly asleep as the air mattress slowly settled back down to the floor.

23116 . . . Commence . . .

19

Professor Perlemutter, in an acre of yellow pajama, sat at the foot of his bed and spoke seriously to his morning visitors. 'I don't blame Damarat for being worried. I give him a lot of credit if he manages to stop with only being worried. Personally, I'm a little nervous. It's a fascinating situation we find ourselves in.'

Ted Ursa, in his Bermuda shorts costume, and Hong pi-Hing, carefully attired in his first western-style suit (double-breasted blue serge), sank into two overstuffed hotel chairs by the bed.

'Fascinating,' Ted agreed. 'The whole higher command of the Alban police force is in a panic. Alba is going to be robbed, looted and invaded, in one swell foop, and they haven't the slightest idea of what to do about it. That, as they've told me several times in the last twenty-four hours, is what they hired us for. I should have become a chicken farmer like my old man wanted me to.'

'Really? Why didn't you?'

'I found out I was allergic to feathers.'

'In Peking last year,' Hong said, 'a man was put in prison for ten years for saying that.'

Ted blinked. 'Saying what?'

'Public speaker stated that for man to live without thoughts of Chairman Mao was like bird to fly without feathers. Man was heard to remark to neighbor that he was allergic to feathers. This was considered subversive remark.'

'I can see the logic to that,' Professor Perlemutter said. He stretched and stood up. 'Well, if I am to start the day, then I'd better end the night,' he said. 'You gentlemen amuse yourselves for a few minutes while I ablute.' He departed, towel over shoulder, and returned within the specified time: shaven, shorn, dressed and alert-looking.

'Good morning,' Ted said. 'How would you suggest we spend the day?'

'Our problem is two-fold,' Professor Perlemutter said, hanging up the towel and putting the carefully-folded pajamas on top of his pillow. 'First: we don't have sufficient detail on how the three elements are to be combined; second: we have no idea of the precise time of the attacks, although we can be sure that they will be soon. What we must therefore do,' he continued, finger poised in the air like a lecturer who has reached his summation, 'is also two-fold. First: prepare for what we know is going to happen; second; seek further information on how it is going to happen.'

'That's kind of a generalization, Professor,' said Ted. 'Could you be more specific?'

The Professor's finger went up again, like a bird dog's tail announcing grouse. 'Let me take one specific example: the problem of the timing. These three events are, as we know, planned to happen in unison; or close together. The theory that the Albanian incursion will happen first to pull our police away from the city has some merit, but in that case the other two events will follow immediately. Now, each of these events must have some necessary preparation. What we must do is analyze what this preparation must consist of. Something, perhaps, must happen the day before the paper mill robbery, or twelve hours before the casino robbery. We must figure out what these things would be and look out for them. That's the sort of thing I mean.'

Before the Professor had a chance to put his hand down, the room door slammed open and three men walked in.

'Put both your hands up,' the man in front said, waving a forty-five automatic around dramatically. 'Way up!'

The second man pointed a large revolver at Ted and Hong, and indicated that they were to perform in a similar manner. The third man closed the door and stood in front of it, his feet firmly planted, and pulled a sawed-off shotgun from under his plastic raincoat.

Ted raised his hands to the heavens like a supplicant priest and looked disgusted. 'Is this one of the things you wanted us to look out for, Professor?'

★　★　★

Smith hauled himself up the rope ladder as if a dozen demons were after him. 'It's good to see you,' he said. 'Help me pull the trap closed.'

'Sure thing,' Peter said, pulling up the ladder. 'Believe me, it's very good to see you too. When are you going to get us out of here?'

'The situation has changed somewhat,' Smith said, peering around the small area. 'Good morning, Miss Blaine.'

'Good morning. Welcome to our living roof.'

'It seems a bit damp.'

'It rained last night,' Peter said.

'Yes? That's right, so it did. So it did.'

'You have a very preoccupied air about you,' Peter told him. 'What's been happening below the stairs?'

Smith shrugged and sat glumly down on the damp roof. 'I've found out what we wanted to know. What the plan is, what the purpose is, and when it's due to start.'

'That's great,' Peter said, squatting on his toes to get down to Smith's level. 'Then let's get out of here and get the information back to Alba.'

'I'll take the last thing first,' Smith said, ignoring Peter. 'The date. The final orders went out last night. The program went into effect at six this morning.'

'What do you mean?' Maggi asked. 'What program?'

'We could, I suppose, call it the 'Rape of Alba,' although that might be a bit dramatic. As of right now, Alba is under attack. The computer gave the word this morning, and Chang Hu, through the computer, is directing the attack.'

Peter's toes started hurting from the squatting position, so he gave that up and sat down next to Smith. 'Okay. Let's hear it. All the details you have.'

'Right.'

'I just found a jar of instant coffee,' Maggi said. 'I'll boil some water.'

Smith nodded his thanks, then passed a hand in front of his face as if to physically organize his thoughts. 'First, there's a good chance that your colleagues, Perlemutter and Ursa, are dead by now. One of the directives the Mind of Chang Hu sent out this morning was an order to put

them out of the way. The idea being to disorganize the opposition. The exact quote Chang Hu used was: 'Cut off the head of snake and the body will die.''
Smith stopped talking and looked at Peter, who said nothing.

'Peter!' Maggi cried. She ran over to him and knelt by his side, putting her arms around him. 'I'm sorry.'

'It's happened before to each of us, and we're all still here,' Peter said. 'Sometimes I think the gods are saving us for something special. Anyway, I refuse to believe it until I see it. What else?'

'The invasion is underway. At least, the troops have started moving. The first border crossing will take place in about an hour. The idea is for the three company commanders that are agents of the Marquis to take their companies across, and see how many other men they can lure across with them. This will cause the Alban Police to assume their paramilitary function and guard the border until the Italians can get there — which is liable to be quite a while.'

'The Italians?' Maggi asked.

'The reason the Grand Duchy of Alba has no army of its own is the same reason it has no foreign policy. By an ancient treaty, all of the Duchy's foreign affairs, including military, are to be handled by Italy. In return, a certain percentage of the income taxes goes to Italy; and if there is ever no male heir to the throne, the Duchy becomes an Italian state,' Peter told her.

'That's so,' Smith said. 'And so the police must defend the Alban border, since Italian troops aren't permitted to enter Alba until requested by the Duke. While the police are busy guarding the border, the two biggest robberies the world has ever seen are going to be taking place simultaneously in the middle. As soon as the robberies are over — or the Italians arrive, if that happens first — the Albanian troops will find themselves without three company commanders, and the high command will have to do some fancy talking to explain what happened.'

'How are they going to be notified that it's time to split?' asked Peter.

'The same way everything else in this

escapade is being run: by using a computer-controlled communications system. In a very real sense, the Mind of Chang Hu is commanding the entire operation. Even the getaways are computer-controlled.'

'How's that?' Peter asked.

'After the robberies, the crooks have to get out of Alba immediately.'

'I'll buy that.'

'And they can't use anything that can be traced or shows up on radar, since they'll be searched for.'

'It makes for an interesting problem,' Peter said.

'The solution is even more interesting. Group A, the boys who are cleaning out the paper mill, are transporting their goods by truck to a hidden pier, where waits an old troop-transport type submarine to pick them and their cargo up. Group B, who is assaulting the casino and assorted jewelry stores and hotels, is to scurry in a convoy of private cars to a secret location and board a dirigible for the trip abroad. Dirigibles, being all rubber, fabric and gas, don't show up on normal radar.'

'Fascinating,' Peter admitted. 'And very

clever. This was all planned by the computer?'

'More than that. Chang Hu doesn't trust anyone. The ships are both to be steered and controlled by the Mind of Chang Hu, from this monastery. By tomorrow, it'll all be over: the Grand Duchy of Alba will be cleaned out and ruined, and Chang Hu will be ready to start his next step on the path to world domination. He will have the necessary money, and he will have proven that the Mind of Chang Hu can be used to control operations of this nature.'

Maggi handed the two men mugs of coffee. 'There's condensed milk,' she told them, 'but I couldn't find any sugar.'

'That's fine,' Peter told her. Smith started drinking his without comment.

'There's another possibility,' said Peter.

'Yes, there is. And the computer — the Mind of Chang Hu — gives it a thirty percent chance of happening. The Marquis doesn't seem to care.'

Maggi looked from one man to the other. 'What's this other possibility?'

Peter told her. 'World War III. If

anything goes wrong with the plan it'll probably be on the side of escalation. With Albania and Italy involved, it could start a major war.'

'Oh!' Maggi said softly.

'It all revolves around that computer, doesn't it?'

Smith nodded. 'Chang Hu trusts its judgment and actions more than he would those of any man. Men can be bought.'

'Well, well,' Peter said, sighing. 'Then there's only one thing to do, isn't there?'

'That's right,' Smith agreed. 'Would you care to assist me?'

'When do we start?'

Maggi asked, 'What's that? What are you going to do?'

'Blow up that damn computer,' Peter told her.

'But . . . there are only two of you. You won't get near the thing!'

'Shucks, ma'am,' Peter said. 'To paraphrase an old Texas Rangers saying: there's only one computer.'

★ ★ ★

After the first two men had left the room, the third man stood by the door and put away his automatic.

'Let me explain to you your position,' he said. 'Not to gloat, you understand, merely in the interest of accuracy.

'To start with, the room is soundproof. The whole hotel is soundproof; that's one of its advertised charms. You can yell all you want to, and all you'll get is hoarse. Next, I'm going to jam the lock from the outside when I leave. With these heavy doors, it'll take at least half an hour for anyone to break in — and that's after they decide they want to. So you'll get no outside help. Also, may I point out that there's no chance of any of you getting loose before the big event. That method of tying — wire around the thumbs and then to the backs of straight chairs — was developed by the Gestapo, and they never had a dissatisfied customer.

'Now, about the, uh, culmination. The string — ' He indicated a child's-toy-type device sitting on the breakfast table. ' — goes to the free side of that hinged pillbox, and holds it up. Under the pillbox, in the glass that we liberated from your ice-water tray, I have poured the contents of a bottle of hydrochloric acid. In the pillbox are two pellets of sodium cyanide. If they should happen to fall into the glass, hydrocyanic acid would form. Since it's a gas, it would bubble forth and spread over the room. One breath of this gas, and *poof*.

'Now we come to the candle.' He struck a match. 'The candle — which, as you see is next to the string — burns at the rate of one inch every ten minutes. I am placing the string approximately half an inch lower than the candle.' He lit the candle. 'Somewhere between four and six minutes from now, the string will catch fire and break. The pellets will fall into the acid. Poof! I believe this method of execution is used by the American state of California because it is so humane. One breath and it's all over. Are there any additions, corrections or criticisms?'

'You're a nut!' Ted said from his chair.

The man stared at him. 'Is that an addition, correction or criticism?'

'Tell me,' Professor Perlemutter asked

from the center chair, 'what do you expect to gain by this?'

'I'm just a poor working slob like everybody else,' the man said, shrugging. 'I'm just doing my job. Well, if there are no further comments, I think I'd best be going.'

Hong sat passively on the third chair, as if he were a spectator at an event that didn't concern or interest him very much. 'May I ask,' he said politely as the man turned to the door, 'what is your name?'

'Why?'

'Obscure curiosity,' Hong said.

'Donald. My name is Donald.'

'Ah!' Professor Perlemutter said, opening his eyes. 'So you're the famous Mister Kott.'

The man glared at him. 'You know me?'

'We have developed some sources of information since we've been here,' the Professor said.

'It doesn't matter, does it?' the man asked. 'Goodbye, now.' He laughed, a sound like gravel pouring down a chute. 'Poof!' he said, going out the door and closing it behind him. They heard the click as he locked it from the outside.

Ted looked around. 'Well, what now?'

Professor Perlemutter struggled with his chair for a few moments and then looked up. 'Can either of you move your chair at all? I find that mine is immobile.'

Ted tried for a minute, struggling savagely against his bonds. 'Nothing,' he finally reported. 'It might be rooted here. And when I put too much pressure on, the wire cuts so deeply into my hand that I can't keep it up. It's a problem.'

'And I,' Hong informed them, 'cannot even get feet to floor. Also, I tried just upsetting the chair, but these old chairs must be very heavy.'

'Seventy or eighty pounds apiece,' the professor agreed.

'Anybody got a watch where they can read it?' Ted asked.

'Morbid curiosity?' Perlemutter asked. 'No, mine's on the dresser.'

'Mine is on my wrist, which is securely fastened behind my back,' Hong said. He sat there watching the candle flame, which seemed to be getting larger and larger every second.

'I can think of two things,' Professor Perlemutter said finally. 'Since our feet are free, can either of you work his shoes off? Unfortunately, I'm still wearing slippers.'

Hong looked up from the candle. 'Shoes? What can we do with a shoe?'

'You can try to kick it through the window. That might let in a little air.'

'Enough to make the difference?' Hong asked.

Perlemutter attempted to shrug. 'Who knows? It might even blow the candle out before it burns down any further. We have nothing to lose.'

'Sorry,' Ted said. 'My mechanical leg's not that flexible.'

'It might be better,' Hong said, struggling with his shoe, 'to toss it at the table; try to upset the candle or the glass.'

'I thought of that,' Professor Perlemutter said. 'I decided against it. Too much danger of hitting the string and dunking the pellets. Now, if we could only kick against the table in some way. It's a light table, and we could knock the glass right out from under the pillbox. No risk of knocking the pellets out, either: it's a deep-sided box. But as for hurling something, it'll have to be at the window.'

'I've got it!' Hong yelled. 'One shoe.' He dangled the loose shoe from his foot like a talisman.

'Fine,' Perlemutter congratulated. 'Heave it at the window.'

'I'm afraid I'll miss,' Hong said.

'Do the best you can.'

'If I throw it at the table,' suggested Hong, 'it would settle the whole thing all at once.'

'I'm not a fatalist,' Perlemutter told him. 'At the window, please.'

Hong muttered a private invocation and whipped his foot around as hard as he could. The shoe took off, describing a perfect arc toward the window. It hit the glass squarely, with a resounding thwack, and bounced off, leaving the glass unmarred.

For a long moment, which seemed even longer to each of them, staring at the candle, there was no sound. Then Professor Perlemutter released his breath. 'It was a good shot. If you can get that other shoe off, I might become a fatalist. In case I don't have another chance, let me tell both of you that it has been a pleasure knowing you. I think I'm starting to babble.'

'Professor,' Ted said, struggling to sit up as much as his wired fingers would let him, 'I don't want to make any promises, but am I at the right angle to kick the table aside if I hit it head-on? I can't tell from here.'

'I would say so, yes. But how are you planning to kick it? Unless that chair's on wheels or you've got a fifteen-foot leg, I don't see how you can reach it.'

'Well, I'll tell you, Professor. It's the fifteen-foot leg. I've been thinking about something we used to do for practice with these artificial legs. Since they work by miniature FM transmitters, we used to practice moving them when they were off the stump. That was only about four feet, and I don't know how far they're good for, but it's worth trying.' Beads of sweat appeared on his brow as he tried to get higher in his seat. Then, all at once, he flipped his body up and down, and the leg was separate from the stump.

Hong stared at the leg, now standing alone in front of Ted's chair. 'I didn't know it was artificial,' he said.

'Let him concentrate,' Perlemutter said.

'The trick is making the leg hop without letting it fall over,' Ted said, tensing his muscles. 'Like this.'

The leg, like a prop from an early monster movie, hopped about four inches in the air.

'It's balanced on the bottom,' he said. 'Let's see if it will go forward.'

This time the leg twitched, then hopped about three inches in the air and one forward.

'That's it! Now to keep it going.'

Slowly, the unattached leg hopped toward the table. Slowly, the candle burned toward the string. Both gaps narrowed, and two men held their breath and thought secret thoughts. Ted had no time for the candle, or for thoughts about anything but his hopping leg.

The leg approached the table. It hopped against the table. It touched the table. It stopped.

The candle flame reached the string.

'Do something!' Hong shouted. 'Once more!'

'It seems,' Ted said between tensed lips, 'that this is the limit of the transmitter. I'll try each of the control motions and see if anything happens.'

The string caught fire, and in a second was flaming from end to end. Professor Perlemutter took a deep breath and closed his eyes.

There was a loud crash.

The Professor opened his eyes. The mechanical leg had fallen over, hitting the table and sending it sliding across the floor. As he watched, the string broke and the pillbox dumped, dropping two blue pellets onto the rug.

Ted was breathing deeply, like a man who has just run a mile, but he smiled broadly at Perlemutter.

'Well,' Hong said. 'Well. Look, the acid spilled.' The glass was upset and a pool of liquid spread over the table, which started to smoke and sent an acrid smell over the room. But it was far away from the pellets, and bore no danger: just a bad smell.

'Now,' Ted said, spacing the words between breaths, 'let's find a way out of here.'

'We have time,' Professor Perlemutter said. 'Now we have time.'

20

Within two hours of the time it was reported that Albanian troops had crossed the border, the police force had mobilized and was heading toward the border in battle dress, leaving only clerical personnel behind. Their job was to halt or slow up the advance until the Italian aid, immediately requested, could arrive. A matter of four or five hours at most, they had been assured.

They found more than two companies of Albanian infantry headed down the Via Claudia toward Graustark, and took up defensive positions on the side of a mountain that blocked the road. The Albanians took up positions on the other side, and seemed content to stay there. Neither side did more than fire an occasional shot toward the other, and both seemed content with the stalemate.

'They know what we're waiting for,' Prefect Damarat, commanding his troops in a colonel's uniform, told his aide. 'I wonder what they're waiting for.'

The man known as Mickey pushed a button.

From the Guard Assurance and Protective Devices, clipped to the belt of each guard at the Royal Alban Paperworks for a ninety-day free trial, came a thin stream of light pink smoke. The guards, and anyone standing near them, dropped to the ground like marionettes with their strings cut. From the Guard Control Master Display Unit in the plant security office came a cloud of pink smoke, and all the off-duty guards collapsed where they stood. Some of the plant personnel who saw what happened decided the plant was under attack. They tried to pick up the guards' weapons to defend themselves, but were also felled by the gas when they got close. Most of the workers just milled around, trying to decide what they should do.

One man called the police, but couldn't get an answer. All the gates and doors were immediately locked.

On the north side of the plant, across

the employee parking lot, a mechanical monster rolled. The fifty-ton charcoal-burning steamroller didn't even pause when it reached the fifteen-foot link fence; it rolled right through, flattening two posts into the concrete. The large brick warehouse was another matter. The machine perceptibly paused before unhinging and splitting open the two iron doors.

Behind the steamroller came a procession of trucks. From the truck emerged a group of gas-masked men carrying machine guns, effectively keeping the curious away. Other men started loading the cartons of special paper onto the trucks.

All the employees were herded into the main building, which had steel doors as a security measure. When they were inside, the doors were closed and welded shut from the outside. Half an hour later, they could hear the trucks pulling away.

★   ★   ★

Tony Fuggio nodded as Benjy the Mug walked up to him. 'Everyone ready?'

'All set to go.'

'Good. See, I told you there'd be no cops around. My friends took care of the fuzz. Go to it.'

'Right.' Benjy walked to the center of the square and raised his hand, then dropped it. Small groups of men, spread casually around the area, picked up from where they were and strolled elsewhere: the casino, the jewelry shops, the various hotels.

The casino was open, but just barely. It was early in the day, and only a scattering of addicts were at the tables. A man entered with a briefcase. Going to the bank window, he put the briefcase down to the side — in front of the locked door — and bought some chips. When he left the window, he forgot his briefcase. A minute later the briefcase exploded, blowing open the door to the strong-room.

The guards were unarmed, and didn't offer any resistance when a group of men, each holding two guns, blocked the entrances and poured into the strong-room. Four of the guards, however, managed to set off the secret alarms. They rang for hours in the empty police station.

The jewelry stores and hotel strong-rooms were all grabbed at the same time. It was done unobtrusively, so unless you entered one of the places, you wouldn't have known anything was happening. Of course, a lot of alarms were set off; but the police weren't responding that day.

All the locations were held while the four safecrackers in the group went around to open recalcitrant vaults. When every safe was clean and all the occupants of the various establishments either tied up or locked in, a whistle was blown in the middle of the square. The group assembled, got into waiting cars and drove casually out of the city.

'Like clockwork,' Tony said. 'We've made history.'

'We ain't away yet,' Benjy growled.

'Wait till you see how we're getting out of the country,' Tony crowed. 'It's a gas.' He broke out laughing. 'Man, is it a gas!'

21

When Peter and Smith approached the entrance to the great hall this time, there were security guards at the door.

'Checking for you,' Smith whispered. 'Don't worry, with that layer of grease-paint on, you'll pass.'

He was right. The guard took a close look at Smith, and then at Peter's Smith-created face, and nodded them both by.

As previously agreed, when they entered the hall, Smith went to the left and Peter to the right. Since neither of them had the technical knowledge to tell which was the critical section of the machine, they were both going to disconnect, disrupt or turn off as much of the Mind of Chang Hu as they could get near.

Peter, with his hood cowling his face as much as possible, picked up a tray of cards from a table and headed towards a large, whining computer block with it. When he got there, he put the cards down and started flipping switches. The lights went off, and Peter hurriedly walked away, toward another machine.

For some time Peter went around doing what damage he could, but the most he seemed able to do was cause a mutter of puzzled annoyance from the technicians behind him. He decided he was in the wrong section, and looked around for a more likely area.

'Attention,' said the loudspeaker in Chang Hu's voice. 'Phase one is complete. Phase two is about to begin. The operation — planned by the Mind of Chang Hu, and you, its faithful servants; and carried out by picked outsiders — is a success. The rest of the plan, carried out directly by the Mind itself, cannot fail.'

Peter looked up and saw Chang Hu pacing up and down on his balcony with a microphone in his hand.

'The future is ours! We will soon have the power to crush all who oppose us.'

From somewhere near the front of the hall there was a sudden stir of excitement. Guards rushed in to a certain point, and the hubbub ceased. Peter, fearing the worst, tried to get a closer look, but was cut off by some tables and some alert-looking guards.

On the balcony a bell rang, and Chang Hu put the microphone down, but forgot to turn it off. 'What's that? He what? Bring that man up here!'

* * *

At that moment, somewhere on the coast of Alba, the man known as Mickey pulled a switch, and a submarine containing a cargo of currency paper and cartoon-named men went on automatic. With no crew, guided long-distance by the Mind of Chang Hu, it submerged and churned its way into the Adriatic.

* * *

The machine next to Peter started to clatter, and he turned to look at it. It was typing out a condition report from the communications van of the Third Company, 12th Battalion, Albanian Infantry; currently visiting the Grand Duchy of

Alba. It was when Peter saw the toggle switch marked TRANSMIT/RECEIVE and the lever marked MANUAL OVER-RIDE that he got his brilliant idea.

★ ★ ★

At that moment, somewhere in the foothills of Alba, Tony the Fudge pushed a button. A long Quonset hut that said *Scrap Metal Bought & Sold* on its side started to split open down the middle. The blue-painted dirigible inside, with its cargo of crooks, money and gems, went under the control of the Mind of Chang Hu.

★ ★ ★

The monk stood between two guards. 'What did you think you were doing?' Chang Hu raged. 'You might have ruined everything.' He peered closely at the monk. 'You're not one of my men. Is that scar real?'

'You don't recognize me?' the other asked calmly.

'Smith! It's you — here!' Chang Hu turned around and screamed into the microphone, 'Kill that man!'

'You devil!' Smith yelled. 'I'll get you!' With a burst of mad strength, he broke away from the two guards and grappled with Chang Hu.

'Kill him! Kill him!' Chang Hu screamed, as the two men fought at the edge of the balcony.

One of the balcony guards, panicked by the screaming, swiveled his submachine gun around. Smith and Chang Hu reeled at the edge of the balcony. Chang Hu broke away for a second, and the guard fired. But Smith had Chang Hu's arm in a grip of steel. As the bullets ripped into him, their impact drove him over the edge, and he pulled Chang Hu with him.

The two bodies fell for a long moment and the guard, frozen with panic, kept shooting.

The bodies hit and bounced off a rack of machinery, followed by bullets.

A long, orange spark ran up the side of the rack and jumped to a far panel, arcing across all the racks between. There was a crackling sound, and the smell of ozone filled the air. Overhead, the great lights flickered and went out. The hall was lit only by sun-bright sparks and flickers of flame as the electronic components of a great brain began to fuse and bubble.

It was, Peter decided, time to leave.

* * *

Somewhere in the Adriatic a submarine began to go around in circles.

* * *

Somewhere over northern Alba a dirigible turned sharply and headed due west.

* * *

On the Via Claudia, an Albanian captain, secretly an agent of Chang Hu, obeyed the last order he had received before the equipment mysteriously went dead:

12989 Advance and surrender at once.

22

Two days later, a bottle of champagne was opened. 'The Italian Navy,' Professor Perlemutter announced, pouring the bubbly into a row of glasses, 'has just rescued a submarine that was going around in a great circle, twenty feet deep, outside Naples.'

'Good,' Peter said with satisfaction. 'They can add them to the crew of that blimp.' He took a glass.

'A sight I'm sorry I missed,' the Professor said to Ted, 'was Peter Carthage with his girl — there's always a girl — dashing across Albania in a Jeep to reach the border before the invasion was called off, so he could sneak across.'

'Personally,' Peter said, 'I'd like to have seen the hotel manager's face when he burst into your smoke-filled room and found you heroes tied to chairs. I'd like to have seen that. Now shut up, the dance is starting.'

'I didn't know you were fond of dance,'

Perlemutter said, as the troop came onstage.

'I've got a friend in the business,' Peter told him.

We do hope that you have enjoyed reading this large print book.

Did you know that all of our titles are available for purchase?

We publish a wide range of high quality large print books including:
Romances, Mysteries, Classics
General Fiction
Non Fiction and Westerns

Special interest titles available in large print are:
The Little Oxford Dictionary
Music Book, Song Book
Hymn Book, Service Book

Also available from us courtesy of Oxford University Press:
Young Readers' Dictionary
(large print edition)
Young Readers' Thesaurus
(large print edition)

For further information or a free brochure, please contact us at:
Ulverscroft Large Print Books Ltd.,
The Green, Bradgate Road, Anstey,
Leicester, LE7 7FU, England.
Tel: (00 44) **0116 236 4325**
Fax: (00 44) **0116 234 0205**

Other titles in the
Linford Mystery Library:

THE SEPIA SIREN KILLER

Richard A. Lupoff

Prior to World War II, black actors were restricted to minor roles in mainstream films — though there was a 'black' Hollywood that created films with all-black casts for exhibition to black audiences. When a cache of long-lost films is discovered by cinema researchers, the aged director Edward 'Speedy' MacReedy appears to reclaim his place in film history. But insurance investigator Hobart Lindsey and homicide officer Marvia Plum soon find themselves enmeshed in a frightening web of arson and murder with its roots deep in the tragic events of a past era . . .

INCIDENT AT COYOTE WELLS

Logan Winters

John Magadan escapes the hangman's noose, but his ride through the Sonora Desert bristles with violence and danger: he's pursued by Sheriff Tom Driscoll's posse; the Corson gang want the treasure which they feel they have been cheated out of; the Yaqui Indians want his horse and his blood. Beth Tolliver knows that Magadan holds the key to free her brother from Yuma prison — and something else . . . and she's decided that Magadan will stay to the bitter, bloody end.

THE MAVERICKS

Mark Bannerman

Despite his innocence, Adam Ballard had served eight years in prison. On release he returns to the Texas cattle ranch where he grew up. But his father is dead and his stepmother has remarried, and the past and present have entwined in a web of violence. Drawn into a bitter rivalry where guns blaze and men are lynched, Adam's past is part of the jigsaw of double-dealing, murder ... and *Mavericking*, the illegal branding of other men's cattle ...